A Day and A Night at the Baths

Other Books by Michael Rumaker

The Butterfly
Gringos and Other Stories
Exit 3 and Other Stories
A Day and a Night at the Baths
My First Satyrnalia
To Kill a Cardinal
Pagan Days
Black Mountain Days
An Immodest Proposal
Pizza: Selected Poems
The Fairies Are Dancing All Over the World

A DAY AND A NIGHT AT THE BATHS

Michael Rumaker

TRITON
NEW YORK CITY

Copyright ©1977, 1979; Intro & Afterword ©2010 Michael Rumaker
ISBN 978-0-9828074-0-8
Cover drawing after a red figure vase from Orvieto, in the Faina Collection.
Triton books are an imprint of Spuyten Duyvil, Inc.

Library of Congress Cataloging-in-Publication Data

Rumaker, Michael, 1932-
A day and a night at the baths / Michael Rumaker.
p. cm.
ISBN 978-0-9828074-0-8
1. Gay men--Fiction. 2. Gay bathhouses--Fiction.
3. Homosexuality--Fiction.
4. Nineteen seventies--Fiction. I. Title.
PS3568.U43D39 2010
813'.54--dc22

2010029302

A DAY AND A NIGHT AT THE BATHS

INTRODUCTION

I began writing *A Day and a Night at the Baths* in early 1977 and finished it by year's end. Although my agent, Patricia Powell, at Harold Ober Associates in New York tried valiantly to place it for over a year, there were no takers until, in a desperate try (I'd been mistakenly led to believe during that time that he'd not be interested in printing any more of my work), I sent the manuscript to Don Allen at Grey Fox Press, then located in Bolinas, California. Don called me the moment he finished reading it and said he would publish it.

The dates are important to mention in order to put the open sensuality in the novel in perspective, that is, pre-AIDS, when male-male sexuality was being liberated from its centuries-long subterranean hiddenness into a visibility if only, in this instance, of the twilit and claustrophobic "freedom" of a bath house.

My attempt in the writing was to shape a language commensurate with that emerging openness, a language vital, alive and cleansed of the language of the past that was all we had had for so long: words of flesh-hatred and shame, language that shriveled body and spirit.

The following, now back in print with this edition, is a sample of what kept me busily scribbling away at my kitchen table in Nyack, New York, for the better part of a year over thirty years ago.

I hurried along West 33rd Street, annoyed with myself that I'd forgotten to take the "D" train and now had to walk the three long blocks from the IND Penn Station stop to Fifth Avenue. My irritation was mainly aggravated by fear: Here I was, 45 years old and, after all these years, making my first trip to the baths.

The baths had always nagged at me as some undone experience in my past gay life. Now, with directions in my head from one of my friends who had been going to these same baths for years (and who, in doing so, had become in my mind a kind of courageous and sexual hero), I walked at a fast clip down 33rd, not so much acting out of impulse as from the realization that the right time to do it had arrived.

I could concentrate on little else. Despite the usual, fascinating swirl of activity of a city street, I blocked it all out, wanting in no way to be hindered in my destination and determined plan. Yet, as I approached the 33rd Street side entrance to the Empire State Building, I spotted a photographer standing on top of the gunmetal wraparound marquee over the entry doors. Below on the sidewalk stood three men in navy-blue suits, looking rather official. I slowed down, curious. What was going on?

One of the three men, pink-faced, blond, was pointing to the high upper floors of the building, his fat nape bulging over his collar as he strained his head back, explaining something to the other two who peered solemn and expressionless where his finger pointed, up toward the tip of the skyscraper's monolithic spear of an antenna which appeared to puncture the low-flying, late-winter clouds.

The photographer was jockeying atop the marquee for a good photo angle, of what didn't become apparent to me until I crossed over 33rd and stood on the corner at Fifth Avenue along with several other street-gawkers who were stretching their necks to stare up at the skyscraper and then stare back down at the marquee on which the photographer was now hunched, leaning and aiming his camera over the edge.

It was then I saw what all the interest was about: at the top rim and toward the center of the marquee was a deep crunch of a dent in the ribbed design of the heavy metal facing, maybe a yard wide and a foot or more deep. The photographer was taking shots of it. Then I recalled that on the news the night before there had been a report that a man had jumped from around the 85th floor of the Empire State and had hit this same marquee with the force and sound, according to witnesses, of "a small explosion." That was obvious in the buckled crater the plummeting body had crushed in the thick metal canopy.

As I turned away, heading down Fifth, my first impulse was to suppose, intimate with suicide among us, that the victim had perhaps been gay. And perhaps, too, first tormented by traditional ignorance, that of the hostility around him, and, finally, his own, was driven to this high place and, in despair, perhaps with unutterable relief, flung himself down from its stark heights.

Whether or not he was gay doesn't matter. Maybe suicides are always victims of passion or ignorance or physical or moral bullying, their own, or others; all of these probably more often than not. "The fittest don't always survive."

What more fitting structure to leap from, then—whatever the reason—than this grim, unyielding slab thrust up from its earthquake-proof base as a vast tablature to dispassionate statistics and figures, this monument of empire, this aggressive memorial to patriarchal rigidities and cold cash? The crunch of a dent in its armor, impressive as it was, from street level, in the scale of the human eye, was no more than a trivial scratch on its thick impenetrable skin of granite and steel. I imagined, as soon as the photographs were taken and everything measured and tallied and accounted for satisfactorily, the scratch would be quickly repaired, easily hammered back into shape as if nothing had marred it. No more than the annoyance of a gnat-bite on the tough epidermis of this skyscraper giant, and as swiftly brushed off and forgotten, as was the larger bite taken out of its hide when the B-25 bomber crashed into it in the fog in 1945.

As for the suicide, simply another disloyal son fallen, among the many daughters and sons who had leapt before, self-sacrifices, nothing more. The film image of King Kong bumping off the cliff-like abutments of the Empire State, circa 1933, flashed into my mind and dissolved. Another child of Kong shot down. Poor bastard, I thought as I quickened my pace down Fifth Avenue. Whoever you were.

As I approached West 28th Street, where the baths

were located, one of the stories my older friend had told me about this particular steam bath back in the 1950s, when I was in my early twenties, came to mind again. Whether it was true or not, it had been the one story, out of many frightening ones, that had mainly kept me away from the baths for so many years in the first place. He had told me that the Vice Squad of the New York City Police Department would periodically send to these baths their "finest": the handsomest and heaviest hung undercover cops who would, dressed in civvies, pay at the door, strip down at the lockers and then go lounge around in the steam room or the dormitory or loiter in the halls. Having surreptitiously daubed indelible (and presumably waterproof) black marking ink on their thumbs, they would wait for some unsuspecting bath customer to go down on them and then would press the ink-smeared thumb on the back of the guy's neck, in doing so pretending, perhaps, a firm and affectionate squeeze, then wait for the next victim.

At a prearranged time, the raiding police officers would arrive at the baths, with several paddy wagons, and announce to the manager that the place was being closed and for all customers to get dressed and leave. As each client left through the lobby, the uniformed cops lined up on either side of the exit would pull back the customer's shirt or coat collar, inspect the nape, and when they found a man with an ink smudge on his neck, yanked him aside and arrested him for "lewd and lascivious conduct in a public place."

Whether this story was just another stitch in the lengthy tatting of faggot fuck-lore, nevertheless, it had been, for me, given my experience with the homophobic laws and their agent-enforcers, enough to know it was *psychologically* true, and that was all I needed to know.

Now that the pressure and uncertainty of police entrapment had lessened somewhat over the years, I rounded the corner of West 28th, my eyes quickly searching for the most venerable, loathed, and affectionately esteemed baths in all of New York City.

The building was not, as my friend had said it would be, closer to Fifth but actually nearer to Broadway. To give myself time, I walked on the opposite side of the street for a little distance. The first things I spotted toward the end of the block—my friend had told me to look for them— were the lighted glass globes on either side of the entrance doors. Their gleaming whiteness, serene, and momentarily steadying, even from a distance, seemed peculiarly in place amid the harsh facades of 19th-century lofts and warehouses and shop after shop of wholesale florists that lined the block. Heartening, too, was a glimpse of early forced French lilacs budding in one of the florist's windows as I hurried by, too eager and unnerved to pause and admire them.

The street, which was jammed with double-parked

trucks and noisy with the raucous shouts and bustle of the drivers, was suddenly ominous to me. My heart, as I backtracked and approached those two globes of light, began to beat faster. I pulled my scarf tighter around my neck in the raw winter wind and, resolved not to turn back, quickly sidestepped my way among the delivery workers and the drivers who lounged against the cabs of their trucks, and the heaps of cases and cartons stacked on the sidewalk, in a street made even more dingy by the heavy, low-hanging clouds moving like blimps over the rooftops.

I could feel my mouth going dry with apprehension as I came to the rounded arch of the entrance to the baths with its grimy, well-worn front step. A small sign in a pane of glass on one of the doors read: BATHS—MEN ONLY. The flat "romanesque" design of the three-story building was as gray and leaden as the clouds moving slowly overhead. The globular lamps were the one cheerful, and hopeful, touch in the entire grim facade.

Even from the street, and with the frosted, mildewed windows of the first floor shut tight, a sharp odor of anti-septic and chlorine hit my nostrils. The building must, I thought, after all these years, exude those smells from the very pores of its stone walls and foundation. I hitched the drawstrings of my handy-sized duffel bag more snugly over my shoulder, took a deep breath and pushed open one of the double-doors.

The initials of the baths were set in tiny green tiles in the floor just inside the entry. I mounted the broad marble steps leading up to the lobby and at the top immediately found myself in the midst of seminaked men wearing nothing but white bath towels around the waist and padding barefoot in either direction across the smooth marble floor of the lobby. The abrupt change in temperature was stifling and I quickly loosened my scarf and pulled off my gloves in the close and dizzying humidity.

Directly across the lobby, behind a plate-glass window at the check-in counter, stood a gray-haired clerk with a pasty, scrubbed-looking face. He was listening impassive through the round vent in the glass to a tall, spectacled youth in levis and windbreaker. As I neared the window I heard the youth shouting in a heated voice, "He stole my watch! I saw him take it but he was out the door and gone before I could stop him!"

"You should've locked it up with your other things," the clerk was saying in a flat, bored voice.

"It was just a cheap watch, that's why I didn't bother. But I'm really pissed."

The clerk shrugged his shoulders and pointed to a sign over the window warning customers to lock up their valuables.

"I know—I know," the youth sputtered, snatching up the rest of his belongings from the counter ledge. "But I'm really pissed—This guy got out the door so *fast*—And I never saw him again."

The clerk wrinkled his brow and turned down the corners of his mouth in a sour expression. "Nothing we can do about it."

Stuffing the rest of his valuables in his pockets, the youth stamped sulkily away from the window.

Intimidated by what I'd just heard, but not wanting to back down, I stepped hesitantly up to the window when the young man had gone. I told the clerk I wanted a room (my friend had suggested that a room was better, if some privacy was wanted, or an undisturbed nap, than just renting a locker), speaking through the vent in the glass, my voice so muffled with tension he snapped, "Say that again?" He glanced at me appraisingly, tartly spotting the obvious first-timer.

I repeated my request and from his expressionless face, without moving his lips, I heard him mutter, "Seven bucks for twelve hours." I slid a bill under the narrow slot at the bottom of the window and the clerk slid back my change and two keys, one for the room and one for the personals box, and a brass disc with the room number stamped on it, all attached to an elastic cord. Then, in a loud grating voice that made me jump, he announced, "KEEP THESE KEYS ON YOUR WRIST OR ANKLE AT ALL TIMES!" and pointed to a sign above my head that said there was a $2.50 charge for lost keys. I nodded I would and he shoved out a long metal box and I took off my wristwatch and dropped that and my wallet into it. I waited a moment since my friend had warned me I might be one of those asked to sign the register, and suggested I give a phony name like everyone else did, but in a growing liberated spirit, I was prepared to sign my real name. I guess I didn't look like a suspicious character, though, or a particularly lucrative extortion victim, since no registry ledger was pushed at me through the slot, the clerk, instead, jerking his head toward a stairwell at one end of the lobby. "To your right. Second floor."

Under his watchful eye I snapped the elastic band of keys around my wrist, picked up my duffel bag and headed for the stairs.

After the bright light of the lobby, I was surprised, when I entered the second floor, to find myself in a long, barely-lit corridor which turned out to be a narrow labyrinth of halls, with the same half-naked men padding up and down or leaning mutely against the walls, faces expressionless but eyes alert, active to every newcomer. There was a curious hush, except for the continuous slap of bare feet on the dark, mustard-colored linoleum and the incessant jingling of numerous keys bouncing off wrists and ankles as the prowling men paced up and down the central hall, some darting down the short narrow corridors intersecting it to peer momentarily into the small rooms. Some of the rooms were dark and others barely lit, doors left ajar, the shadowy occupants, a few totally naked, reclining invitingly or appearing to rest or doze.

Straining my eyes up at the walls in the gloom, trying to make out the arrows pointing to the various room numbers, I was distracted by those who passed me holding erect penises provocatively and in offering through their towels. Not to mention the heat which, evidently rising from below, was more humidity-laden here on the upper floor. I had had timid doubts about baring myself in front of all these strangers, but now was eager, in the choking heat, besides feeling conspicuous in my street outfit, to shed my clothes as quickly as possible.

I followed the arrowed room numbers as best I could in the dim light (I wished, giddily—the heat, I guess—that I'd brought a flashlight in my duffel bag!), stepping over piles of damp and discarded towels near the attendant's station. Although it was a weekday, the place seemed pretty busy, the attendant nowhere in sight, perhaps off changing the linen in a recently vacated room.

Finally, after several minutes wandering and backtracking, I at last found Room 208, the last door at the very end of one of the short corridors where there were perhaps eight rooms in all. I had a lot of trouble with the key in the lock, not only because of nervousness and the heat (I still had on my sock hat and winter coat), plus the distractions of a number of men prowling up and down and around me in this very narrow offshoot of the corridor, but also because, catty-corner, the door across the hall was wide open and lying naked on the bed, delicately fondling himself, was a slender Oriental youth who looked to be no more than 15 or 16.

I was about to ask this lad if all the locks were tricky (I was still too intimidated to ask any of the naked strangers circling around me for assistance, and none offered any), when the loose-fitting lock finally opened (they undoubtedly got a lot of wear and tear) and I stepped into my room.

Turning on the wall light, which turned out to be a 10-watt bulb inside a broken glass shade, I glanced around the room which was really a cubicle, with just enough space for a bed. The air had a sour musty smell, as did the whole second floor, mingled with pockets of other, more pungent odors that I was only able to identify later. Hard to tell about the condition of the one sheet and pillow case in the weak muddy light. There was a battered metal ashtray bolted to the wall at the head of the single-size mattress which, when I sat on it, turned out to be a thin pad of foam rubber atop a wooden platform joined to the wall.

The cubicle was really just a partitioned enclosure of a dark brown plastic-coated paneling of wood, the walls of which, especially over the bed, were smeared with hair oil and grease and what looked like lubricant stains. The "ceiling," several yards above the eight or nine foot partitions, was actually the ceiling of the entire floor.

With the top of the room open I could hear the noises and voices in the rooms in the immediate vicinity. The most clear and distinct sounds came from the other side of the wall in the cubicle next to mine: the firm steady rhythmic hand-slapping of flesh.

Feeling faint from the combination of heat and excitement, I quickly got out of my clothes, draping them on the hangers on nails in the wall, and wrapped the bath towel around my waist, knotting it in a convenient hole that was torn in one comer.

The piercing voice of the clerk in the downstairs lobby cackled electrically over the intercom loudspeaker, "Hey, *tell* that guy in 234 his time's up—He shoulda been out fifteen minutes ago."

"Yazz, I *awready* tol' heem," came the voice of the attendant in response, and then louder, evidently to another attendant somewhere else on the floor, "Hi, Santos, tell that *flaco maricón* in two-tree-fawrrr to get the hell out!" A distant, "Hokay!" was shouted back. "I tell heem one more time."

I sat on the bed again, lit a cigarette and, to fortify myself and wet my dry throat, took several swigs of coffee from the bike thermos I'd brought with me in my bag. A little calmer, I leaned over from the bed (not having to reach too far in that small cramped space), opened the door and peered out.

In his darkened room the Oriental youth was lying

with his long slim legs spread and still casually fingering his genitals. My first impulse was to go over and assist him, but I thought, green as I was to the place, I'd better take a look around before anything else.

A number of men came up to my door, stopped, peered in, looked briefly at me, a few groping themselves under their towels, then padded away again. Usually they went directly to the youth's door where they remained staring in a little bit longer than they had at mine. Curiously, they got no response from him.

Cooler now, emboldened a little, and very curious, along with a rising erotic under-rush, I stubbed out my cigarette, careful to make sure it was out in the ashtray and, even though it was a metallic container, poured a little coffee over it from the thermos, my immediate and uneasy reaction to the very flammable look of the cubicle.

I got up from the bed, knotted my towel more tightly around me, and decided I might just as well plunge in.

But first I had to find a urinal. With my system working overtime in accelerated anticipation, what I needed immediately was to take a powerful piss.

I joined the throng of men patrolling the halls, feeling exposed but less self-conscious than I expected now that I was undressed and towel-draped like everyone else. In a few of the rooms I passed there were sometimes two or three men sitting side by side on the bed, backs against the wall, smoking, quietly conversing, laughing together

     A Day and a Night at the Baths

in cozy camaraderie.

In one such room there was a couple sitting facing each other on the mattress. The one nearest the door turned his head as I walked by and asked, with an inviting smile, "Wanna make it a threesome?"

The thought of sex with two others in such a tight space didn't at the moment appeal to me, so I shook my head and said, "Know where the john is?"

He hitched a thumb down the hall. "Straight ahead, babe. Maybe catch you next time."

In the next cubicle, one of the few I'd seen so far where there were two men love-making with the door open, a young man with starched blond hair, too neatly coiffed, a bit too radiant to be natural, was saying, with a very toothy, sparkling smile, to the top of the head of another youth just in the process of ducking down between his outstretched legs, "*Bon appétite, chéri.*"

I found the toilet just off the dormitory at the rear of the floor. It was a room without a door, two graffiti-scratched stalls—"Water Sports Room 307" "Rm 235 for terrific S&M" "FF me in dorm 1 a.m."—and an old porcelain-lined urinal trough. As I stood at it, the soles of my bare feet tacky on the damp tile floor (that made me cringe a little inwardly, realizing what I was standing in— I'd seen a few men walking about wearing Japanese bath sandals, but the majority of the customers went barefoot, and I had, out of a sense of wanting to "belong" I expect, decided to go barefoot, too), a man came in and began smoothing and adjusting the waves of his sandy-colored hair in the large mirror behind me. He was perhaps in his mid-30s, a broad-featured, roughly handsome face, with wide shoulders and a solid build. Even through his suntan (he had the expensive physique and looks of someone who could afford a mid-winter vacation), you could see the freckles on his face and those scattered down over his shoulders, and this made him somehow even more attractive. He exuded health and vigor and his substantial poise suggested he was used to getting what he wanted. He took no notice of me and I was too shy suddenly to speak to him but was pleased to look, glancing over my shoulder as I urinated, trying not to be obvious or to stare too much, practicing a little poise myself.

Satisfied at last with the look of his hair, he left the mirror and strode purposefully out of the lavatory. Off his left hip, the knot of his towel stuck up jauntily like a cocky white flower, emblem of a certainty I envied.

Leaving the toilet I paused, with some trepidation, just outside the dark doorway of the gloomy cavernous dormitory, where my friend had told me most of the "orgies" took place. I peered into a huge, L-shaped room, filled with row after row of what appeared to be the same platform beds as the one in my cubicle. Scattered throughout the dark were the orange points of lighted cigarettes and, judging by the odor, marijuana joints. A few faint blue bulbs in the ceiling cast a cold wan light and, except for an occasional small square of glassed-in light of very low wattage set in the base of a few beds near the entrances and at the crook in the "L," and the dully glowing red of the EXIT signs over either entrance, the large space was in almost total darkness.

My heart began to beat with apprehension, and as my eyes adjusted to the dimness I could see the vague shadowy outlines of bodies sprawled here and there on the beds, most of them naked, some curled in sleep or lying on their backs, legs spread. Others roved restlessly back and forth among the beds. Close to the door, on one bed, the dim figure of a man knelt between the legs of another, fellating him in the "Chinese-style," his torso thrusting up and down in vigorous arcs from the hips.

In the area where the room formed an elbow I could make out a sudden flurry of movement, ghostly and im-precise forms floating together eerily in a rapid surge of activity it was too dark to see clearly. My imagination expanded vividly, however, along with my timidity, and I backed away from the entrance for the time being, deciding first to check out the steam bath itself, and the swimming pool.

First thing was to find out where they were located in the building. I turned and walked down the hall and stopped a youth and asked him directions. He looked at me askance—there were signs on the exit doors reading

"TO BATHS" but I was still too disoriented to follow them or understand whether they meant up or down or left or right. "Down those stairs," he said. "And then the stairs down from the lobby to the basement." I thanked him and moved to the stairwell he indicated and started down.

As I entered the fourth and very lowest level of the baths, I saw, to my right, the massage room, like the cubicles also dimly lit, with the masseur himself, a bulgingly muscled man in white tank top and sharply creased cream-flannel trousers, his powerful hands expertly manipulating the oil-glistening thighs of a client reclining on the massage table, his legs the only part of him visible since his upper torso was hidden beyond the door.

In front of me, in brighter light, stretched the swimming pool, a large blue oval at the head of which two stone gargoyles, at either side of the metal stairs descending into the pool, fiercely spouted wide-lipped streams of chlorine-reeking water.

The turquoise water looked inviting, and I imagined it was comfortably heated, but something about indoor pools, the enclosedness, the dank chemical smell of them, has always turned me off, and I decided not to go in.

Naked and sleek as an otter, a young man, the only one, swam effortlessly around and around the perimeter of the pool with long lazy pushes of his arms and easy froglike kickings of his legs.

The bleak tiled walls of the huge room dripped with perspiration. Amid the strong and nostril-stinging antiseptic odors was a cold, earthy cellarlike smell of fungus. I half expected to see mushrooms sprouting from the walls and high ceiling, even between the tiny white tiles of the floor itself, which was sweaty and slick under my bare soles, so that I stepped carefully to keep from slipping.

In wireback chairs by the water's edge several men sat, undraped, drinking coffee from paper cups and languidly watching the swimmer circle the pool. One of them, a slim black youth, small pearls of water still glistening in his hair from a dip in the pool, sat with a leg propped across his thigh, tucking his keys inside the elastic band snapped round his ankle.

So that was the secret! The constant tinny jingling of the keys dangling from my wrist was a nuisance—I understood now what a belled cat felt like. I sat down in a vacant chair and slipped the keys on just above my ankle for a snugger fit, the flesh thicker there than on my arm, inserting the keys and brass disc securely inside the band, just as I had seen the youth do. As I passed him on my way to locate the steam room, my keys no longer jangling, I thanked him silently. He glanced at me briefly but appraisingly.

Up on a shelf near the ceiling a color TV set blared, but no one was paying any attention to it.

The steam room was between the shower and drying rooms, behind a thick gray-metal door, unidentified, except for a small sign warning customers not to stay in longer than thirty minutes at any one time. When I pulled open the door and entered I understood instantly what the sign meant.

A blast of sulphurous heat squeezed all the air out of my lungs and caused me to stagger back against the door. The dense fog of steam was so thick and the heat of it so concentrated that I didn't venture far into the room. I stood just beyond the metal door, the soles of my feet burning, riveted to the hot concrete floor.

My friend had told me, and I had heard from others, that people had sex in here, but I couldn't imagine the possibility of standing there, even inert and inactive, a second longer, let alone exercising myself in even the mildest and quickest form of love-play. It was all I could do to simply stay on my feet, and breathe.

Through the billowing vapor I glimpsed snatches of musclebeach physique: a sweat-shiny muscle-bound chest or a pair of gleaming well-developed buttocks—evidence of a heartier species—which quickly disappeared in the rolling clouds of steam. These men must have the blood of tropical climes slogging through their veins, I thought. But my curiosity melted in the caustic fumes and infernolike humidity. Not waiting to see what type of erotic action played itself out here, I began edging my way backwards, groping for the door, my lungs gasping for cool, dry air. I shoved the door open and stumbled out, gulping the moist air in the passageway as if it were from the most arid desert, and by contrast to that of the steam room, it was.

When I got my breath back I glanced again at the sign on the door of the steam bath and couldn't imagine anyone staying in there as long as thirty minutes. In that time I'd be carried out delirious, or dead, the latter more likely. Five seconds had been enough for me.

I unknotted my towel and hung it on a peg in the drying room, then crossed the passageway and entered the showers, longing for some soothing cool water on my body.

About a half dozen men were standing under the streaming nozzles in the open, brightly lighted room. I found a vacant showerhead beside a youth whose curly hair was the color of dark honey. As I soaped myself I glanced around the room, cautiously at first, but seeing that no one was paying any attention to me, except a few in the most casual and flat-eyed way, I grew less self-conscious and more determined in my gaze.

Under the row of showerheads across the way, two lads were showering together with the intimate and careful gestures of lovers, although they may have met only a few moments before. One was soaping and meticulously cleansing the genitals of the other, and then they reversed their roles, the other doing the same for his partner. They spoke quietly together and had a physical closeness and, in their touchings, a respect, that was lovely to watch. They now were lathering each other's back, taking turns, their hands gradually working themselves down to wash between each other's buttocks.

Most of the men in the showers had a robust and healthy pink tone to their skin, many of them in superb physical shape, hardier specimens, evidently fresh out of the steam room and undoubtedly, from the glow of their skin, capable of enduring longer stays there than I had.

I turned, under the water, in such a way as to see more clearly the youth showering beside me. He was lightly sudsing the flat pectoral muscles of his honey-tanned chest, the points of his grape-dark nipples distending under the caressings of his fingers. His eyes, beautifully shaped, were light green, set in a handsome, intelligent face which sported a neatly trimmed mustache. Those eyes, the color of the sea off Fire Island on a sparkling green day, looked around him with a level clearness but at nothing or anyone in particular. His soapy hands moved down slowly and lingeringly over the lean, corded muscles of his belly, then ever so gradually farther down to the thatch of deeper-honeyed pubic hair, his fingers straying lightly through it, then the tips of his fingers playing down slowly over his prick, soaping it carefully in deft small whorls of lather. It was then his eyes, unself-consciously, without embarrassment or the leer of the tease, looked out at us, from one to the other, as if to say, Look, I want

     A Day and a Night at the Baths

to show it off to you. Like the naïveté of a boy proud to display his most gorgeous possession, to share the look of it, the pleasure he had in it. And rightly: It was well-shaped; even more shapely as it thickened and lengthened like a blood-snake in his caressing fingers. I watched, not furtive, likewise unembarrassed in my looking, content only to watch, as seemed the others, including the two lads who also paused in their showering to look over at the youth.

Now his eyes, with their absorbed smile of serious pleasure and play, held the hint of an inward secret of barely contained happiness. They were also eyes that looked out at those of us in the shower room and clearly said, Isn't this a wonder?

In the aura he exuded—it seemed to fill the steamy air—I felt my own to be a wonder as well, and sensed the others did, too.

It grew in his hands, the long slender stalk of a rosy flower blooming out of his fingers: the shower water was like rain; his strong brown hands, the kneading earth; his face, sun-touched, and all our faces, beaming down on it, the encouraging suns that emboldened it to lift its head in a sure and sturdy bud-swelling. And it was no more than that, only to show it to us at its full and best advantage. He grinned at us and then turned his back, hunching his shoulders and ducking his head under the streaming water, and began to rinse off.

Now really refreshed, and encouraged, not only from the cold shower but the image of the young man like a healthy roseate radiance lighting up my eyes, I crossed over to the drying room, got my towel and slinging it over my shoulder, went out to see what the sauna was like and dry off.

As I balanced my way along the narrow precarious space between the edge of the pool and the wall of the sauna, I had a sudden sense of the place and thought, Here, we were our naked selves, anonymous, wearing only our bodies, with no other identity than our bare skins, without estrangements of class or money or position, or false distinctions of any kind, not even names if we chose none. Myself, the other naked men here, were the bare root of hunger and desire, our prime need to be held, touched and touching, feeling, if only momentarily, the warmth and affectionate response of another sensuous human. Here, was the possibility to be nourished and enlivened in the blood-heat and heartbeat of others, regardless of who or what we were. Nurturing others we nurture ourselves.

The sauna was just off the swimming pool and, through the chicken-wire safety glass of its door, I could see that it was a large, redwood paneled room, free of even the tiniest smidgen of steam so that the interior and those inside, despite the aged and heat-darkened walls, were clearly visible.

I pushed open the door and entered an atmosphere

of intense but very dry heat. Several men, fresh from the showers like myself, were rubbing themselves down briskly with towels. One man lay stretched flat on his back, eyes closed, on the uppermost wooden tier. I sat down near the door on the second slatted platform and let the heat, billowing from large vents in the walls and from slits beneath the wide, step-like tiers, dry my skin. Within moments the warmth penetrated deliciously to the marrow of my bones (and through the metal of the keys around my ankle, too, so that I had to roll them higher up my leg away from the direct blast of heat pouring from the vent against my feet and lower calves). The sauna was definitely a more hospitable environment to me than the steam bath.

As I sat there, beginning to feel, for the first time since my arrival, genuinely relaxed, I looked through the large plate-glass window—like the glass in the door, also embedded with protective wire—and watched the men outside sitting on the wireback chairs by the pool. The TV set was still on and still ignored. The loungers were observing, more often than not, as I was, in a casual, relaxed manner, the variety of men parading naked between the steam room and the sauna, or the occasional nude swimmer slipping into the pool.

I looked for the black youth who'd shown me the trick with the keys but he was nowhere in sight.

The men didn't stay long in the sauna, only spending

enough time to dry off quickly, then departing in the direction of the upper floors. I remained a little longer, tentatively rubbing at my wet legs with my towel, reluctant to leave, myself and the man on the upper tier, who appeared to be dozing, the only ones remaining. Then the door opened and a tall, very thin man in one of the short blue cotton robes I'd seen a few men, mostly portly, wearing, entered the sauna, rubbing at his scrawny stomach with a towel.

He glanced at me timidly with eyes sunken in his thin, boyish face, then peered up cautiously over my shoulder toward the sleeping man. His salt and pepper hair was clipped in a crew cut that was now growing out, and he came and planted himself directly in front of me, very carefully drying his genitals now, giving me a tiny smile that was both shy and also subtly leering at the same time. It made me uncomfortable, as well as the fact that he was standing so close to me in the all but empty room. I nodded to him and went about drying my feet, giving my toes a great deal of attention, but I sensed him move closer to me. It was difficult to ignore the elaborate, circular slow drying of his groin, his thick penis rubbed red now. Then his hand, with thin spidery fingers that startled me, reached into the space between my legs. I seized the hand gently and firmly moved it out of reach so that it brushed back clumsily along my inner thigh.

"Thanks," I said, in my most unrejecting tone, "but not right now."

I looked at him fully now, surprised at his gesture, at the insistence of his stance, since, short a time as I'd been at the baths and inexperienced as I was—and it may have been naive of me—I sensed that people didn't make out in the sauna: that seemed to be reserved mainly for the upper floors where it was dimly lit, and more conducive, more "private," in shadows.

I saw now he had an almost emaciated physique; that in spite of his boyish features, he was a much older man: his skinny legs sticking out beneath the robe were knotted with varicose veins and bruised and bumpy with age.

For a moment the soft snores of the man lying behind me were all that was heard in the room.

Then, withdrawing his hand, his lips became rubbery and began working uncontrollably. I thought he was about to cry. "I'm sorry," he said.

"Don't be sorry," I told him, as gently as I could, beginning to feel like a real heel. "You don't have to be."

I was about to reach out and touch his shoulder when, his features screwing up tighter in a pinched, pleading way, his voice self-pitying and whining, he said, "I always do the wrong thing."

I withheld my hand. "Don't be so hard on yourself," was all I could say, and I knew it wasn't much. I actually wanted to smack him, for whining, for begging. He reminded me of a part of myself.

Instead, I looked at him quietly. He had stopped

rubbing at himself and stood abjectly with downcast eyes that occasionally flicked nervously to the door, as if he was fearful someone might enter.

His skeleton figure and childlike face made me think of long-term patients I'd seen in mental hospitals, faces frozen in time, emotionally stuck in some long ago part of their lives.

"Some man punched me last time," he bleated, casting a wary glance out the sauna window, "for touching him."

"Some guys are like that," I said, standing up on the tier and knotting my towel around my waist. "They don't know any better. This is my first time here, but I guess that can happen."

"I always make mistakes," he said. Then, after a pause, "I'm sorry."

I stepped down onto the wood-slatted floor beside him. "Don't keep saying that." This time I put my hand on his shoulder.

"I'm sorry," he repeated, his head ducked down on his chest.

It was hopeless, and really getting me down. I gave his shoulder a squeeze, and the boniness of it felt frail and vulnerable under my fingers. "Come on, buck up," I coaxed, and actually wanted to pull his head up and straighten his shoulders, but it seemed like years of apology had twisted and bent his neck muscles, the bones of his back, in permanent submission. All I said was, "Try to enjoy yourself," and was embarrassed and downhearted at how lame it sounded.

I went to the door and stepped out into the much cooler air of the pool area. On a sheet-draped resting lounge beneath the TV set, a blond-haired youth, no more than 17 or 18, and evidently strung out on a bad drug trip, lay curled tightly, his hands pressed flat against his face. A young man, several years older, crouched beside him, speaking quietly, trying to comfort him, his hand making calming movements on the youth's shoulder.

I climbed the long wide flight of stairs slowly to the second floor and returned to my cubicle.

Leaving the door ajar, I lay back on the mattress, the pillow behind my head, and waited. Several men poked their heads in the door but didn't linger. My towel was still draped modestly over my middle and I wondered if I should remove it, or at least uncover myself partially. I tried to figure how I could arrange my arms, my legs— perhaps I should cant my hips—in a fetching manner. I was never very good at seduction: Hollywood had been no help to a sprouting gay lad.

My friend had told me that if you lay on your back at the baths that meant you wanted to be sucked; if you lay on your stomach that meant you wanted to be fucked. I wondered what would happen if I laid on my side?

I also wondered if I should leave the light on or turn it off—I'd noticed some of the men reclined on their beds in total darkness, perhaps with the notion of enhancing mystery or, more likely, with the intent of erasing real or imagined physical "flaws." Either way, it was a definite enticement. But, still somewhat uncertain in the newness of the place, and also out of a grudging sense of honesty— "What you see is what you get"—I decided, for the time being, for all the use it was, to try my luck leaving the light on. And, for the present, too, to lie propped up in a partial sitting position with no attempt at anything other than being as comfortable as I could.

I closed my eyes, feeling a sudden wave of tiredness, and after only a few moments was aware that someone was standing in my doorway. When I opened my eyes I was surprised to see it was the sandy-haired man I'd seen earlier arranging his hair in front of the mirror in the toilet. He only stood in my door for the breadth of a second. Obviously knowing exactly what he wanted (and could, as I said, have whoever he wanted), he gave me a quick, sizing-up sweep of his eyes from head to toes, then turned on his heel and walked snappily to the door of the cubicle next to mine, where so much flesh-slapping had been going on when I arrived.

I thought maybe I'd do better to turn the light out after all, but decided the hell with it.

From within that cubicle I recognized the cheerful, somewhat sultry but surprisingly energetic voice of my neighbor, "Hello-o-o-o, welcome to my place."

The perky flower of the towel-knot riding on the hip of the sandy-haired guy moved quickly in and disappeared from view.

The door shut and after a moment or so I heard hushed quick whispers and low laughter. The acrid herbal pungency of marijuana smoke suddenly smarted the air. Presently the funky, cock-cheese odor of Lockaroma wafted over the wall.

"I'm so stoned," I heard my neighbor breathe, in a raspingly pleased and utterly laid-back voice.

I settled into my pillow and shut my eyes again to sharpen my hearing. No matter where your ears turned there was the sound of some fresh erotic adventure here. By this time, the resounding smack of an open palm flat on firm buttocks was heard, the pair next-door evidently losing no time getting down to it.

No rest possible now. I opened my eyes and stared at the wall opposite, which separated me from my neighbor, listening contentedly but with keenly attuned curiosity. Perhaps I would learn something. Then I noticed midway down the wall two small, carefully drilled holes precisely spaced to fit a pair of eyes. I propped myself up on my elbows. Pinpoints of light from the adjoining cubicle gleamed through the tiny holes, drawing my eyes like bees to the bright pistils of a flower.

I crawled to the foot of the bed and put my eyes to the holes, feeling like a Japanese courtesan, in a samurai movie, who has wet her finger to make an eyeball-size puncture in the tissue of the rice-paper wall to watch the lovemaking in the adjoining room, keeping an eye on a lover perhaps.

Only these walls were plastic paneling, streaked with the oil and grease of lovers' hands, and urgent love-scrawls of KY-sticky fingers. These old stains were like graffiti tracks of passion, more legible and vivid than any written word or crude sticklike drawing on a lavatory or public wall. They evoked the cries and breaths and urgencies of all who had ever come in secret yearning to this cubicle.

There was, of course, no finger-moistened hole, here in this cubicle at least; only these two tiny openings perhaps drilled by some enterprising former occupant through the thin partition, one for each curious and voyeuristic eye.

I put my face close to the wall and looked through the holes and now not only heard but saw: a sandy-haired head bobbing vigorously up and down, then the smooth, very white flesh of an inner thigh (my first glimpse of my neighbor), its muscles ropy as the leg flexed up tight, the sinews relaxing as the leg unbent slowly.

"I'm wrapped so loose," the voice of my neighbor murmured dreamily.

I realized suddenly that my door was open and, carrying still-strong remnants of the behavior code of the world outside the baths and not wanting to be caught as a peeping-tom, scampered off the bed and slammed it shut.

I sprang back and knelt again at the peepholes, gluing my eyes to them, moving my head from side to side and up and down, straining to get a better angle of vision in order to see more.

But not much more than this was to be seen: a tanned freckled hand coming into focus, clasping a muscular white shoulder—positions had been changed in my brief absence—and after several minutes of hard steady thrusting, a blur of swiftly interchanging patches of white and tanned flesh, accompanied by the sound of the muted thwack of hip-flesh slapping against buttock-flesh. There was a thin high cry of exhilarated keening. Then the sound of a heavy body collapsing exhausted on another, and all was quiet. The partially seen figures of both men had disappeared now below sight-level.

I pulled my eyes away from the peepholes, reclining back on the pillow, and leaned over and swung the door wide open. Arranging myself in what I hoped was an attractive position, I lifted my terry-cloth towel away from my thighs and glanced eagerly out into the hall.

Over the way I saw the Oriental lad lying on his side, staring across the hall toward the door of my neighbor. His body was leaning forward, his face concentrated in a tense, listening expression. Our eyes met and he, for the first time, broke into a broad impish grin of sly complicity. I grinned back, too, slid off my bed, locked the door behind me and went across the hall and into his room.

He lifted his head and turned his shoulders as I entered, lying now, in a rapid flip of the hips, in one of the favored house-positions, belly down. Close up, he even more definitely had the slender body of a boy, graceful in its lines, suggestive of the dancer. I enjoyed particularly the delicious curve of his spine to the dip at the small of his back with its barely visible dimples. His buttocks were small but as firm-looking and rounded as spring melons, without a trace of even the fuzziest hair. Long, elegantly thin legs were spread relaxed and wide on sheets that looked as dingy as mine in the turgid light of the wall lamp. (His cubicle was similar in every detail except that the bed faced in the opposite direction.) His skin was the color and texture of smooth ocher clay. Peeping out between his legs, at the under-cleft of his buttocks, was the pleasantly surprising contrast of his scrotum, its pink plums tufted sparsely with curling black hairs.

I offered him a cigarette and as I held a light to him I could see his face more clearly in the flame of the match: buff-featured with longish silken jet hair, cut bob-style, framing his face. But also in the match-light, I was perplexed to see that there was something old and muddied in his features, a flatness of expression, something totally private and protected: the street-sharp, and smartened, face of a gutter angel.

The spontaneous elfin grin he'd flashed at me just a few moments before now left no trace on his features, as if some totally different person, a stranger, had taken possession of the cubicle in the few seconds it had taken me to walk across the hall.

He thanked me for the cigarette, and there was such a sound of weariness and indifference in his voice, that whatever initial desire, and hopes, I'd had, quickly evaporated. He regarded me briefly and in the narrowness of his eyes there was a flat cold expression of embitterment, the tiny curl of his mouth in a smile giving a famished twist to his lips.

Puzzled, feeling tricked by the brief openness of his grin of several minutes before, I stood rooted where I was, no longer wanting to move closer to him.

He twitched his hips, grinding them into the mattress, throwing a look over his shoulder that was both defiance and challenge. Something curdled in me. I felt myself withdrawing, had already left the room, even though I remained fixed where I stood, held by the hypnotic poison in his eyes.

Maybe it was anger at finding himself stuck here on this cheap, sagging mattress in such a sunless, airless place that had hardened those eyes, that had already etched his face with the acid of disillusion and lost hope. Not wanting to be there and yet not able to tear himself away. Even in so brief a time at the baths I had begun to realize the possible acute addiction to the place, there were so few alternatives.

I asked him if he came here very often. His mouth was almost a snarl. With an angry turning away of his eyes, he made some unintelligible reply.

"This is my first time here," I said, and felt like a dope, not knowing how to leave.

He snorted and crushed his face into the pillow. "It won't be your last," came his muffled voice.

"I really want to have a good time ... " I began again, feeling even dumber, but seeing that he lay quite still without responding, I faltered and grew silent. What it was to be as he was, not only here but in his home, in the place that he came from—I knew nothing of that, and not knowing how to ask, backed off.

After a moment I said, feebly, "I hope you have a good time, too," and edged out of the room. He made no move or sound.

I returned to my cubicle.

I sat on the edge of the bed, beginning to feel really blue. Perhaps my instincts, although grounded in fear, had been right. Perhaps I had made a mistake in coming here. And adding to my down mood was the depressing pall of the odors of amyl and butyl nitrites, the capillary looseners and orgasm heighteners, like a combined smell of stale popcorn, rancid peaches and sneaker crud, that hung like a heavy reeking cloud in the air in all the endless corridors throughout the baths. Torn popper wrappers and broken ampules were strewn outside my door on the hallway floor.

The nicotine and marijuana darkened walls, which appeared not to have had a brush of fresh paint since the place was built, seemed permeated with that particularly inert, greasy odor of poppers. Wherever you went, the musky chemical smell of it was constantly in your nostrils. I sat on my bed breathing it in, unwillingly, and longed for a breath of fresh air. Except for the shut window in the toilet, I hadn't seen any other windows here on the second floor. Later I would go up to see what the third floor was like. Perhaps there would be a window there, however small, where I could stick my nose out and breathe something other than the cold, kerosene smell of amyl.

I kept thinking about the Oriental youth, like someone held there against his will, an exile, trapped in that cubicle across the hall for the rest of his days, his desire gone meaningless, only the spasms of habit remaining, returning him again and again to this spot; someone damned to haunt these hallways forever, even long after the building collapsed in decay and dust or burned to the ground in cinders, the aborted and beaten spirit of him prowling always—And how I have always felt myself like a person in exile; and other gay women and men to be in exile, anonymous in the cities, inconspicuous in the windowless cubicles of baths such as this; banned from the rural places—or if not escaped yet, in hiding there, among leaves, among roots; cut off from dances of the country ground, from the stories and songs of the Green Spirit they used to sing, the grass-roots music they danced to in other times, celebrating resurrections and sanity processes of earth, the mother, caressing the skin of her in affection of her increase and abundance; combing, with their dancing, protecting and keeping lovely, the grasses that are her hair.

I mean the gay selves in all of us, the double-heart and the double-mind in two-way seeing, whether maimed or shriveled or vigorously surviving and growing, the delighted elf and fairy energy in the thriving child-play of existence—all banished people now.

I stretched out on the bed, clasped my hands behind my head, and gazed up at the ceiling. I began to squirm uncomfortably. The sheets, besides looking soiled in the bad light, felt scratchy and moist under my skin. Perhaps the mattress was alive from its last warm body.

I imagined the sheets, the skimpy mattress, enseamed with lice, "cooties d'amour," as they are called, love bugs. The shapely posteriors parading by in the hall I imagined rampant with hepatitis, the penises that flamed with passion flaming with spirochetes as well; and scabies, and yaws, and all the other parasites carried here, along with desire, by the sailors of love from every port of the globe, the lonely and flesh-hungry from every corner of the nation and from every borough in the city; carrying here centuries-old infections of the fathers, their gay sons infected hosts, carriers in blind desire of invisible flesh-eating stowaways on bodies innocent of contaminating, and, in imperative yearning riding out the fears of infection, driven to this contagious harbor again and again, myself among them now, there are so few unrestricted havens, no ports free of the contaminating fathers.

My legs and arms began to itch, more from imagination I expect (I'd seen the attendant changing the linen in vacated rooms), but I scratched energetically anyway. As for clap and syphilis ... I forbade myself to think about that either.

Tomorrow will be better, I decided, what with A-200 and other drugstore lice-killers, and the Gay Men's Health Project in Greenwich Village ("Free V. D. Examinations 691-6969"). After the pleasures of Venus, trust to the availability of penicillin.

I nestled my head more comfortably in the pillow and continued to stare up at the ceiling. With so many matchwood cubicles jammed together, ceilingless, with no windows or fire escapes visible, the open stairwells without fire doors excellent ventilating shafts for shooting flames, I began to feel a creeping sense of claustrophobic panic, one of the several but not overriding fears that flashed in my mind when I first entered this dark and crowded second floor. And there were so many men here loose or high on drugs and alcohol, and there was not only a great deal of cigarette smoking but pot smoking as well, a carelessly dropped butt or roach ... But I didn't want to think about that. What good would it do anyway? I pushed it out of my mind, wanting only to look forward now to the erotic adventures I'd heard so much of and had fantasized about. I longed for them to become actual.

Then, up on the ceiling I spied—or at least could make out only vaguely in the bleary light—what looked like a fire-sprinkler outlet. I couldn't be sure and narrowed my eyes, lifting myself up from the bed, but still couldn't be certain what the small round object set in the ceiling was. Finally I gave up and lay back, deciding it actually was the nozzle of a sprinkler—Surely they would have such a system here, in such a crowded and tindery place.

I had seen several fire extinguishers hanging here and there on the walls in the corridors. I thought of the gallons, the tons of water circulating through the pipes on the premises, in the shower room, the swimming pool, the steam bath itself, and that thought, dubious as it was, was comforting. Better to believe that than not enjoy myself, in spite of well-grounded concerns. I leaned back against the pillow, reassured, letting my uneasiness recede back into the depths of consciousness.

More immediate uncertainties swarmed forward in its place however: I hadn't yet participated in any of the experiences that were my main reason for being here, and that I could plainly hear going on behind the walls of all the cubicles surrounding my own.

Slapping in the room next-door began again. I roused myself. I really wanted, myself seeking, to get out and join the other seekers walking the halls, see what that was like, and also discover who was there in the other rooms on the rest of the second floor, and then go up and take a look at what the third floor was like.

As I started to get off the bed I was aware of someone standing in the doorway observing me.

A youth with cascades of dark glistening curls was looking in. He was wearing one of the short light-blue cotton robes, the hem well above the knee, a sash tied at the middle. The skin of his face and arms was so white it glowed in the dimness of the corridor.

He stood peering down at me for several moments. I was perplexed what to do on this first promising bathhouse venture. Wait for him to make the first move? Lift my towel away with a leer and grope myself provocatively as I'd seen other men doing in cubicles I'd passed? But I knew that I would make an awkward and somewhat ridiculous tempter. Instead, I smiled and simply said, "Come on in."

He entered without a word, closing the door behind him, and sat beside me on the bed. He had magnificent blacklashed eyes. "Been here long?" he asked. I shrugged my shoulders. "I don't have my watch. A while, I guess."

He gazed slowly up and down the length of my body, then leaned over and kissed me. He had a mouth for kissing. Reaching under my towel, he fondled me in a relaxed, easy way.

"Got any poppers?"

I said I didn't, that I'd never used them. He looked surprised. "Not ever?"

I shook my head and was about to tell him of my addicted past, how I didn't want to take chemicals of any kind any more, but decided this wasn't the place, or the moment, to go into that.

We kissed again, easy his kisses were, as easy as his hands playing over my body. After a few moments I suggested he take off his robe. He said, "I guess that'd be a good idea." A look of momentary hesitation in his eyes told me he was a little shy about taking it off. I wondered if it was only simple shyness with a stranger. Perhaps he had scars, or was deformed in some way? Would it have mattered? A man with some "deformity," a harelip, say, or one who's a deaf-mute, has an appreciation and kindness that's often missing in those with more standard, off-the-rack bodies.

When he slipped off his robe I could see it was only that he was a bit on the fleshy side, just a big healthy solidly fleshed lad who'd let himself go a bit. He had the build of a wrestler.

Once he was naked I laid him back on the bed and the whiteness of his body surprised me again: it wasn't a dead pallid shade but a rich creamy whiteness. Its glow added wattage to the meager light bulb and seemed to brighten the room considerably. I made a mental note to myself that on the next trip I'd bring a bit of rosy-colored tissue paper to put over the bulb.

I slid down on the bed and began to explore his body with brushings of my lips. Under his chest and down the sides of his ribcage, beneath the skin and gleaming through it, ran fine even whiter veins of flesh, delicate traceries of snowiness that fanned out against his skin. I touched his nipples with the point of my tongue and, like the tips of peony buds, his tits protruded instantly against the luminescent sheen of his smooth skin, ruddy early flowers in a field of snow.

He asked me to kiss his nipples some more. They were hard in my mouth and he moaned as I kissed them. "Bite them," he said. "Bite harder," he gasped, rolling his head from side to side on the pillow, his eyes shut tight. I took one again in my mouth and, gingerly, bit a little harder. His nipples became slender red palps between my lips, my mouth a dragonfly threading stamens.

"Ah, that's good," he sighed.

After a few moments he made a move to go down on me, but since I felt no urgency, lively as I was, up all rosy and eager, I laid his head back on the pillow. He gazed at me with that look of suspension between sleep and wakefulness.

I glided once more down the icy brilliance of his body, closing my lips over his scrotum, obliging him so nicely he warned me of imminent explosion. I hurried to paddle the tide of rising peony flush now running like fine rivers of heat down the whiteness of his flesh, flooding there to gorge out the bulging knot, bringing with it the pungent snap of riverbed minerals, and cartwheeling silverfish in millions, the outrushing tide suffusing me in a sunup of invigorated rosiness.

After I groomed him neatly and leisurely, we lay back for a few moments in each other's arms. He kissed my mouth, cooling it a little. He whispered in my ear, "If this secret gets out, it'll revolutionize the world." I laughed. "It will," I said.

We lay quietly for some time, then he put his face close to mine and thanked me. He got up and put on his robe. "I'll probably see you later."

"Yes," I said, although I knew we probably wouldn't.

He smiled, touched my face and went out the door.

I stopped briefly in the toilet again to rinse my mouth at the sink and spit into the urinal trough, in a probably futile but at least mind-settling attempt at rudimentary hygiene. Next time I would bring some mouthwash to gargle with, and a toothbrush.

An excitement of sperm-lust, whiffs of it bleachy in the air, aerated me with an agitated impulsion to feed close. I visualized the minutest trace of blood in the sea stirring sharks to glide along the inky tentacles of its faint trail hanging in the water to ultimately zero in on the kill in a thrashing and frenzy of feeding. My face burned with a thrill of delighted shame in the comparative image, my teeth were that sharp, possessed as I was by original hungers.

Boldly, with no backstroking, I swam into the next open doorway I came to where I sighted a live, breathing body afloat on its back on a bed of rumpled sheets, its waving blood-red tendril an appetizing lure.

His name was Paolo. From Brazil, he said. A fish from far waters. And from a very good school, too: he spoke excellent English. He looked like an exotic breed from the equatorial upper-classes, he had such a sleek and privileged look and, the joint he was toking aside, an air of confidence and insouciance of manner that only old and habitual money can buy. With wavy iron-gray hair, he wasn't young but appeared expensively youthful, the body trim and tanned and well taken care of. He exuded a relaxed and antique Latin American charm. I found myself thinking about monkey gland transplants. Around his neck hung a small discreet crucifix inset with diamond chips on a fine gold chain, and I thought of the small bands of Portuguese and Spanish thugs who brought syphilis to South America in the Name of God and wondered if he was their true heir. I also wondered if one of the more light-fingered customers here, in an unguarded moment during the throes of passion, might not relieve him of his cross.

My shark teeth sharpened.

Another toke, and he told me, conversationally and with a merry, amused glint in his eye, pleased to accommodate, that he was storing up a bladderful for "a nice guy" who'd stopped in shortly before me and had extracted the promise from him.

"Said to drink a lot of water and he'd drop back later. I hope you're not into that yourself because I wouldn't want to disappoint him. I'm not much into water sports but he seemed such a sweet guy."

I assured him I wasn't either and that he could fill up as much as he wanted. Not that I wasn't willing to experiment, but I didn't add that.

"Thank goodness," he smiled, relieved. "No fun having to get waterlogged a second time. I've been wearing a trail between here and the water cooler as it is." Chin pressed on chest, tamping probing fingers over a belly flat as an ironing board, he said, "I'm getting a bit swollen now, don't you think?"

"And down below, too," I added, rakish, baring my teeth.

"More there than here," he said, patting his belly affectionately.

With the most gracious smile, he offered me a drag from his joint. I declined but opted for a few tokes of the real thing which he allowed with a satisfied smile and a generous parting of his thighs.

He was wearing a cock ring so unusual I bent down very close to inspect it. Faint and delicate designs of looping snakes, heads biting tails, were etched in the silver band, as worn as a family heirloom. A rough leather thong of rawhide clamped the metal hoop tight behind his testicles, the thong, which he'd evidently dampened, perhaps on one of his trips to the water fountain, shrinking tighter and tighter as the rawhide strip dried against his body heat, bulging his balls out like Valencia blood-oranges, his prick increasingly ramrod stiff from the slowly squeezing pressure. It looked excitingly painful.

My nose sharpened as I nudged around purple veins swelled to bursting in a nest of ink-black pubic hair crinkled with gray the gloss and texture of watered silk. He had a scrubbed unerotic smell with a strong hint of Aramis. My tongue itched for an unadulterated taste of salt-fresh blood. Slipping a finger below the thong, I touched an anus loose and yielding for easy entry.

He brushed my cheek with well-manicured fingers. "You're a sweet guy, too," he breathed in a marijuana basso. He sighed profoundly. "Do with me whatever you like."

And I did, patiently and thoroughly, not as a shark I found out, because, even though I made use of my teeth, it wasn't blood I eventually drew. The sting of it, uncontaminated by perfumed soap or heavy cologne, was a welcome shot of carnal reality.

Straddling between his legs, I glanced up at one point and caught Paolo smiling over my head, a sparkling grin like a movie star's splitting his face. At first I thought it was ecstatic bliss and was just about to congratulate myself on my performance when, hearing distinct heavy breathing just over my shoulder, I swung around and spotted several pairs of eyes staring intently and curiously through the crack in the door. Kneeling at the foot of the bed, my butt up close to the door, my flanks exposed, so to speak, I felt very vulnerable and, reaching back with my arm (and hating my priggy rudeness), closed the door tightly.

Paolo pulled a long puss but I soon put him in a better mood, not saying a word but getting back to the work at hand until, with a kick of his legs in the air, he let out the squawk of a rooster getting its neck wrung, his arms and legs flapping, then fell back on the mattress in utter collapse. Diminished now, his cock ring slid off and dropped on the bunched up sheets between deflating testes like balloons slowly leaking air. The metal hoop lay there like a coiled and useless outsized earring.

He blew me a genteel peck from his lips. "*Obrigado*," he murmured, "*Merci*," and dropped his eyes demurely, a polite way of saying, 'I think I'll just rest now.'

Crawling off the bed I stood up and slipped my towel around my waist. I said I might stop back later and say hello if he was still there.

"Please do," he said, and pulling another joint from beneath his pillow, lit up again. After expelling the smoke in a thin, quick cloud, he said, arching his eyebrows, "*Santa Iansa*, I hope that *bicha avec les goûts particuliers* gets here soon. I don't think I can hold off much longer."

I hunched my shoulders and giving him a commiserating smile, wishing him speedy relief, reached a hand behind my head, flipped an imaginary top hat at him and, peeling out of my shark skin, strolled out the door.

After another trip to the showers I began to realize that constant showering after every escapade could really shrivel up the skin and decided next time I'd bring along a bottle of Aapri Body Satin Lotion—"Leaves Skin 'Sauna Soft' and Refreshed."

Then I climbed at last to investigate the third floor, the uppermost part of the baths. I paused near the top of the steps and looked back down, seeing all the way down the steep flights of stairs to the marble lobby floor two stories below. Towel-clad figures moved up and down on the deep-grooved rubber treads of the steps, sharp under bare soles. The long downward rush of stairs was broken only by the wide landing leading to the second floor, from which I'd just climbed and up to which a man in lumberjacket and levis, evidently just arrived, was trudging.

Wearing nothing but a sweatshirt with YALE in big block letters across the chest, a tow-haired youth with a pink, protein-fed face, open, innocent, the face of a remote pilot peering with dreamy, abstract eyes out of jet bomber plexiglas, jogged onto the third floor landing and bounced athletically past me down the steps, hands stuck straight out at his thighs, fingers tapping air, a loose, quick spring on the balls of his feet as he tripped blithely on down the stairs, pink genitalia jouncing.

On a metal folding chair on the landing just outside the doorway sat the attendant, a heavy-set, middle-aged black man in short-sleeved white cotton shirt and trousers, a benign and passive-faced guardian of the third floor entrance whose main job it was to show customers to their rooms, supply extra towels when asked for and change the linen on the beds after customers left. I soon discovered he was also involved in some moonlighting of his own. (I expect his salary wasn't much—the attendants relied on tips and my friend had suggested that a quarter would be "adequate"—and so this little business on the side that in a few minutes I would chance on, must've helped fatten his weekly income, and then some.)

I glanced at him as I passed and he nodded curtly, neither friendly nor unfriendly. He looked like he had worked here for years, at this same station, sitting on this same folding chair, perhaps even in the days when the baths were not predominantly gay—in palmier days of the neighborhood, according to my friend, when it was an exclusive Turkish bath and clubhouse for wealthy, and presumably white and nongay, men only. He had the kind of blunt, grizzled face that looked, in its guarded ruggedness, tactfully unseeing, surprised at nothing.

Once through the door, I was immediately aware, in contrast to the floor below, of the "lightiness" of the area. Looking down the first long narrow corridor just off the entry, I was relieved to see, at the far end of it, the small square dusty light of a window. I started toward it, hoping I could open it and get a breath of fresh air.

On the way, I passed many closed doors, silent within (they seemed to rent all the second floor cubicles first before letting out the third floor ones), but a few of the doors were open and I slowed my steps to glance inside them. Other men passed me, circulating in the same round of cubicle-cruising as on the floor below, but here the atmosphere seemed quieter, a little less frantic and close-quartered, the space not as broken and abbreviated by the short alleylike halls; perhaps quieter, too, because there wasn't the proximity and activity of the downstairs dorm. Here, the cubicles were lined either side along the simpler layout of three very lengthy corridors stretched parallel from front to back of the building.

One man lay on his bed wearing nothing but a jockstrap; another wore scanty, pastel briefs; another, black leather briefs with a zippered pouch. Several were nude or posed with their towels arranged in such a way as to definitely arouse curiosity. A long leanly sinuous man was totally bareass except for a pair of cowboy boots, the blunted points of which jutted out beyond the door so that you couldn't help but brush them as you passed, which I guess was the main idea.

In the next cubicle a man lay flat on his belly, his legs extended in a wide "V," a foot-long plastic dildo, pointing straight up, and pointedly leaning against the partition beside his bare buttocks.

The attendant suddenly pushed up behind and around me, escorting a newcomer, a bearded young man wearing a black leather jacket and form-fitting leather pants, both studded all over in curlicue designs made of brass rivets. A stiff black SS-type military cap was perched over his shaggy blond curls.

The attendant unlocked a door just ahead and turned on the light. It was a supply room with shelf upon shelf stacked with clean towels. Tacked up on the inmost walls of the closet were vivid color photos, cut out of nudie magazines, of naked women, huge-breasted and sleekly curvaceous.

Surrounded daily by the constant sight and noise of so many undressed men engaged in so much same-sex activity, the photos, exaggerated as they were, perhaps were a reminder, helping the attendant keep a grip on his own preference each time he paid a visit to the closet.

"How's your supply?" I heard the man in leather drag, sounding like an old hand, say to the attendant as I approached.

The attendant glanced at him quickly with lifted eyebrows. "You *know* I always got a *good* supply." His thumb, like glossy teak, riffled up a stack of neatly folded towels.

The blond youth grinned. "Lemme tip you now," he said and snapped out a bill, sliding it into the palm of the attendant, who then transferred it deftly into his hip pocket. He reached up between two stacks of towels, palming a small brown envelope, barely visible for the fraction of a second as he withdrew his hand, then folding the envelope neatly into a clean towel, he handed it to the young man.

"This is good *strong* stuff," he said in a low, confidential voice. "A *good* buy."

He gave a tug at the light chain, locked the door behind him and continued escorting the young man down the hall to his room. Several heads turned at the clump of the heavy boots, their militant stomp sounding until the two rounded the corner at the far end of the corridor and disappeared from sight.

A white-haired man, perhaps in his early fifties, stood naked just inside the shadowy doorway of his cubicle. He stared out at me with a flat, stolid face, the points of his eyes concentrated in unblinking and earnest solicitation. He was fingering his testicles and manipulating them in a flapping, beckoning manner. My eyes met his and I nodded but kept on walking toward the far window.

Slumped on his bed against the wall, staring with

youthfully handsome but bored, indifferent eyes at the partition opposite, sat a young man with short-cropped blond hair, a narrow waist and the wide, sloping shoulders of a swimmer. The model of a "good school" type, he appeared out of place here, like a fantasy ghost of the 1950s, roaming seamier halls than the ivy-clad ones of that time.

When I glanced in he dropped his gaze, staring down at the folds of the towel in his lap, his square-jawed muscles tightening.

"You into Crisco?" he muttered.

I stopped in the doorway, not sure I'd heard him right. Sparkle of a cock ring through his parted towel, long in a thigh as sleekly muscular as a frog's.

He jerked his head to the corner of the cubicle where, in the center of the small nightstand, the only object on it, stood a one-pound can of Crisco, the smooth whorls of its snow-white surface as yet untouched.

Seeing my hesitation, he looked up at me carefully from under his brows. "There're lots of things you can do with it."

I had an image of myself, and him, smeared head to toe with the stuff and rolling around entangled in greasy sheets, then my being handcuffed and tied spread-eagle to the bed with slip-resistant rope, a prospect that for the moment was a turn off.

I also imagined him, clothing his nakedness, dressed

in a striped school tie, red corduroy vest, gray flannel trousers and a navy-blue blazer with dull metallic buttons—Another dead and respectable ghost, among so many, my head was so filled with them—But all ghosts now and pretty much at rest.

I shook my head. "Not right now."

Then, slow and quiet-voiced, "Thanks for stopping by anyway," he said, and turned the humorless gaze of his eyes again to the partition.

Maybe another time I would be more adventurous, but for now my immediate tastes ran to the raw and unadorned flesh, without additives of any kind.

As I walked on, I wondered if the advertising department at Procter & Gamble was aware of a new and exciting use for their product? (Or, for that matter, if the makers of Chapstick knew that their lip balm applied to the lips beforehand lubricates the glans as an aid to deepthroating? One more reason to "Never Go Out Without It.")

Many of the rooms, as on the second floor, were in total darkness, perhaps because, dim-watted as the lights were (the frosted shades appeared to be broken in a majority of the rooms), a bare light bulb was a bare light bulb and, like the one in mine, irritating to the eye in such a cramped space.

The darkened room certainly served as an allurement, enlivening curiosity, suggesting mystery. Perhaps for some it was a disguise, as in one room where I could make out the stretched out figure of a very old man, propped on his bed on one thin withered arm, the door just barely cracked and the light not on. Concealed in shadow, perhaps a pathetic attempt at trickery to make him appear a little more "desirable," to fool someone, out of desperate loneliness, into entering, if only for a moment?

In a very few cubicles, there glowed soft orange and red bulbs. I wondered if these had been installed as a fluke, or because of a shortage, on the part of the management? Perhaps the occupants of these more invitingly lighted cubicles had had the foresight to bring their own bulbs, unscrewing those supplied by the baths and replacing them with their own more romantically tinged light.

Instead of the rose-colored paper perhaps I would bring a pretty light bulb on my next trip.

From somewhere down one of the long hallways I heard a cracked, pleading voice, the grainy voice of an old man, crying, "Could somebody tell me where Room 306 is? Please help me find Room 306."

There was a bustle of footsteps and the attendant saying in an annoyed, weary voice, as if he'd done this now for the umpteenth time, "This way, pops. 306 down here," and an apologetic cackle from the old man as he said, "Damn if they don't keep moving it on me. Thank you, thank you."

Did such old men live here? Did the owners of the

baths have an arrangement with the social services of the city, cut-rate prices for homeless and elderly men during slack times when the management wanted to fill up cubicles? Or perhaps it was only that they chose to be here, like everyone else, in such a spry and busy sexual atmosphere.

I stopped at an open door where, stretched on his bed, his handsome head propped up on the pillow, lay a huskily built dark-haired man with very symmetrical features, a wide neatly clipped mustache and a smartly cropped haircut, giving him the overall appearance, *sans* work boots, levis and Sears cheap flannel shirt, of a Christopher Street clone. He was wearing only a very brief tangerine towel (undoubtedly one he had brought with him since, except for a few washed-out pink ones, most all the men were wrapped in the ordinary, threadbare terrycloth ones). Around his neck was a thin chain with two delicate gold pendants. He looked like a commercial for aftershave lotion.

I put my hand on the doorknob, thinking of the dial of a TV set, and smiled.

"How are you?"

"I'm fine, love," he said. His teeth were very white.

The broadcasting school blandness of his voice encouraged me. I clicked the knob and went in. I'd always wanted to meet one of those perfect television specimens up close.

I stood a foot or so out from his bed, not wanting to get too familiarly near, tentative as to approach, glancing with uncertainty into his dark-lashed eyes. I ventured a hand on the flat muscles of his chest, lightly dusted with fine black hair. It met no resistance. The trace of a smile played over his lips, his black eyes watching me. I stroked his chest farther down, running my hands over his well-developed legs which were also covered with soft sooty hair. The whole of his body was in excellent shape, like he really spent a lot of time on it, exercised or swam a lot. I longed to find a scar, even some imperfection, however slight. But there was none. Perfection. And what can you do with perfection? Stick it up in a museum, I guess, or a video screen. He looked like a commercial for Jantzen swim trunks.

I lifted the pendants of his necklace but the light, as usual, was so bad I couldn't make out what they were.

"One's a good luck charm," he offered.

"And the other?"

"That's a Hebrew symbol."

I told him I liked the necklace. It seemed the most real thing about him, but I didn't tell him that.

He put a hand on my arm and said to me, in the most agreeable way, but in a tone that suggested I was wasting his time, "I'm just resting, hon."

"Sure," I said. I began thinking of the unexpected possibilities in the numerous cubicles throughout this floor and the floor below. I suspected the lump between his legs to be a stick of roll-on deodorant.

He was so at ease and pleasant-natured, I thought he must have smoked some dope, but I smelled none in his cubicle, not that that meant anything. I decided to change channels.

"Enjoy yourself," I said and placed my open palm lightly on his chest for a moment. There was a definite heartbeat.

The smile you could trust clicked on. "Thanks, love."

Leaving his cubicle was like walking out the front of a cathode tube.

I came to the end of the first hallway at the front of the building where the small grimy window was inset in a boxlike casement. I was glad to find I could slide it open, and did, sticking my face out as far as I could through the narrow opening. Even the soot-laden and chemical air blowing over the city was a relief from the oppressive atmosphere of perspiration and genuine and artificial smegma smells, the rank underground odor of the window-sealed building. I longed for a whiff of the flowers on display behind the plate-glass windows of the wholesale florists up the street.

Pedestrians were hurrying by on the sidewalks below and the block was jammed with slow-moving traffic because of the double-parked trucks at the curbs. To the north, the Empire State Building glowed with a granite light in the silvery reflection of the fast-flying clouds that were lightening up now.

As I leaned out the window I felt an unseen hand casually squeeze my ass in passing, but I didn't turn to look, just kept breathing in the cold air in deep drafts.

After a few minutes I left the window and wandered into the middle hallway, moving slowly toward the rear of the building, my head clearer now. Passing the shut door of one cubicle I could overhear husky voices inside, one saying "*That* was all *right*," and the other responding, "Yeah, put that in your roach clip and toke it." Somewhere, another voice, commanding in good humor, "Don't you *dare* cum yet." Over the wall of another cubicle a few doors down, still another voice in a resigned, factual tone, "No use knocking yourself out. I can't help you, man—It's dead."

From the attendant's station the staticky voice of the clerk down in the lobby was heard through the intercom speaker: "Room 325, tell that guy in there his time's up," and the attendant shouting back from somewhere over in the next hallway, "325—OK!"

At intervals, from someplace close by, came the sharp, repeated, almost desperate whisper of, "*Suck it!*"

A little farther on, a half dozen or so men were standing in a knot, listening intently outside the door of one room where the sounds of violent slapping and punching were heard. I squeezed my way around them and a couple of doors down discovered a youth perhaps in his early twenties, fair-skinned with dark blond hair. Slenderly muscled, he had a boyishly appealing face. He was lying flat on his back, not in a relaxed way, but holding himself in a rigidity of apprehension. His round eyes had a look of fright in them, almost of frenzy, as if he expected the very worst to happen. He was clutching his penis through his towel in a tight fist, staring out through the doorway with the expression of a frightened, frustrated boy about to cry.

Perhaps, like myself, this was his first time at the baths. Probably he'd been lying there listening to the energetic punchings going on in the room down the hall. Perhaps it was that and something else, something maybe that he carried with him all the time and had brought here to the baths, which only magnified it in these surroundings. Maybe he really was waiting for somebody with the look of a punisher.

His expression was so poignant I stood in the doorway for a long moment, not knowing what to do or say. Probably better just to go away. Humanism can be inhuman.

In spite of his display of nudity and the knuckle-whitened hand clenched at his crotch, he appeared, from the tension in his face, in no way to be awaiting some delightful erotic occurrence. If anything, he looked afraid of getting beaten up, or murdered—not uncommon fears in the backs of the minds of most gay males. But here that seemed, though not impossible, at least less likely to occur than elsewhere. Given the whole gamut of playful as well as vicious variations practiced at the baths to the widest and fullest degree, every satisfaction of taste and desire was possible and, giving assent, probable. If his pleasure was in servility and the trust of sadistic control in pain, perhaps the shaggy blond-haired youth in the SS cap I'd seen a few moments before would come strutting by.

If it was that, and if it wasn't ...

I lifted my hand to him in a kind of wave of greeting, not knowing what else to do. I asked him if he was all right.

"I'm okay," he said, his voice strained. "Just resting."

"Are you sure?"

"Yeah—Sure." His eyes clearly told me to let him alone.

"Take care then," I said, and walked on, having seen clearly in that moment, beyond all speculation, a glimpse of an old and passing self in those wide, frightened eyes; passing on to instinctively protect the recently acquired space of this different self I felt myself becoming; no longer wanting, or needing, to be contaminated that way again, in early fear become reflex, in chronic worry, in habitual defensive alert: not able to help him either, or at least not knowing how, not yet fully healed myself, not yet the healer.

So many of us frightened here, I thought, so many

faces that passed me with the look of urgent and perilous need that seemed to have nothing to do with sex, or the reason for being here.

In a dark corner a slow firm hand pushing a groper's fingers away, dissuasion enough. There were doors you stopped at where the occupant, without speaking a word, with a turning away of his eyes, or the all but barely perceptible curl of a lip to one side, told you plainer and louder than words to get lost.

And there were those I found whose cubicle you entered, deciding to risk it, who, when you touched them, slapped your hand away or turned their shoulders abruptly. Rejection learned here, as in other gay male cruising places, as readily as acceptance. But that helps oil it, and you're off, direct, busying on in search of the next and, with hope, more open and accommodating flower. Eros isn't stingy. But the unwanted are here, too, and the too wanted. The too handsome and the not handsome enough, the ugly and deformed—even one youth struggling about the halls on aluminum crutches, his twisted legs strapped in metal braces ("There is no end to desire")—And the very old and the very young, they, too, are here. The cock-teasers, too, I saw, who lured you and when you approached, aroused, pushed you away roughly, often with a sneer. Macho gays were here who needed, all ways, to be on top, to "win" at all costs, where the partner doesn't count except as a used and humiliated participant in their petty glorification. The scrawny with no chins and the chubby with too many; those with pipestem legs and those with the legs of weight lifters. The small cocked, the big cocked, the slender peckered and the stout pricked; the loose-assed and the tight-assed, the beer-bellied and the flat gutted; and all those who give better than they get—All here with all their fantasies and desires, their little lies and big ones, their bent dreams and passing straight dreams and dreams of soaring and airy gayety—The beautiful on the outside who are poisoned inside; and the physically ugly who keep close and quiet a loveliness within that many are blind to, often even themselves—All prowl these dreary dim halls with the same purpose and search: to find, surprised, behind the monotonous row on row of cheap plywood doors, endlessly opening and closing, the heart's desire and the awakener of the heart; the miracle of a barely imagined paradise, here in this dingy smelly place, heavy with stale body odors and decades-old perspiration of lust-sweat, and fear-sweat, and ashes of spermfire that encrust the walls and floors and ceilings from all the century-long years of those who have searched here in unspeakable pleasure and pain (for there is unspeakable pain here, too); searching patiently and tirelessly to discover, in sly and passionate ambush, in the litter and stink of this hidden away bathhouse in a floral market street of the city, a tiny glint of the shy and elusive flower that enfolds the secret and the meaning. And each of us brings that here, furled tight in the unconscious, in the cellar of need, prowling for it in this house where sunlight is not, nor moonlight, nor nurturing air and moisture, our vision purblind, slaking our thirst on ashes.

I leaned against the wall between the doors of two cubicles and closed my eyes for a moment, envisioning whole stretches of seacoast of briny and sunny sensuality, their beaches and environs unpolluted by attitudinal poisons; gay children, lesbian and gay peoples, giving only to sisters and brothers, giving the others nothing, depriving them of their energies, depriving them of their bodies, cleansing the flesh of patriarchal syphilis, of the poisonous gonorrheas of imbalance, the rape and violence of toxic maleness run riot; all the sons and all the daughters no longer crippled, no longer born blind, no longer living blinded, deprived and hungry; now depriving, cleansing, purifying flesh and spirit, the unpolluted energies returning strong, eros protecting those close and obedient to its ways.

Envisioned great green parks, genuine *play* grounds, too, of open pleasure, wildernesses of nudity given over to sensual disobedience, with all the obedient freedom of mutually consenting and courteous erotic play in praise of happiness and well-being, in praise of ourselves. Playgrounds without chain link fences penning in children, and never again children hanging by the neck from poisoned trees within such holding pens, legs kicking in the unimprisoned wind. And every hometown in America with a free public bath, but, unlike this one, airy and light, open to everyone, where purified mothers and other women teach the girl-children and purified fathers and other men teach the boy-children, in gentle massage, in merry bubble-winking strokes of beginning awareness, in the double cleansing of purification and fleshly acceptance, in encouraging right and clean and courteous ways, the kindliness of our bodies, to know and respect the incredible instrument of sensuous joy, received and given, the body is; and then none can ever be unkind to another, learning in ceremonies of bark and root and wild flower and herb, in open air peoples' baths, to scour ourselves and each other, perspiring in sweat lodges to sharpen vision again, sweat out the poisons, for how we will be with each other; and the gay children live again, and all the children live in us, emptying the mental hospitals and doctor's waiting rooms, depleting the populations in prisons, cutting the death-by-broken-heart rate to zero.

This vision lasted only for a moment since the clamor of perpetually jingling keys, the dull sound of restlessly moving feet sliding up and down the linoleum halls, the sharp cries and gasps and thwackings of flesh in the cubicles around me, didn't allow even the briefest moment of escape.

From over the top of the partition I was leaning against voices drifted:

"I'm fucking my dentist to get my teeth fixed."

"I did the same once with a proctologist when I had my anal warts."

"The pig."

"He said the exercise was part of the treatment."

Sputtering, snickering laugh.

"Did it help?"

"Well, you just tasted the results."

"Not bad. My thanks to Doctor Proctor."

A long sigh.

"What's a poor gay boy to do?"

Opening my eyes, I saw through the open door in the cubicle directly across the hall a redheaded youth spread-eagled on his bed. His skin was the color of ripe peaches. I crossed over and leaned on the doorjamb. After a few moments, aware of me standing there, he turned pale blue eyes to look at me.

"Want company?"

His face was expressionless, studying me. Light coppery eyelashes. He looked me up and down and finally said, "I could use some."

I entered the cubicle and stood beside him, laying a hand on his shoulder, stroking it. His skin had the furry velvet of peaches. Not changing his spreadlegged and belly-down position, he extended an arm and reached under my towel, feeling the heft and size of me, his eyes measuring, weighing. Satisfied, he jerked his head in a "come on" way and sank his face on the pillow again.

I unknotted my towel and let it fall to the floor and climbed onto the bed, kneeling between his legs. His eyes closed slowly, his mouth opening to shape a wide "O" as I ran my fingertips tickling down his spine and played them over the small of his back. The muscles of his buttocks quivered like dartings of wind over water.

He stretched his legs wider on the bed, one leg now pressed flat against the wall, the other jutting off the mattress, stiff and tensed, toes curling and uncurling. I traced a finger along the downy cleft of his buttocks, his anus exposed now to my eye, red seed in a freshly halved peach.

From my kneeling position, I leaned over and swung the door shut.

AFTERWARDS, I WALKED DOWN THE HALL, swinging my arms, whistling, on my way to the showers again. Heads turned to look at me. Then I realized the sound of whistling was unusual here, that I hadn't heard so much as a single tweet anywhere in the whole building since I got here. Or open, hearty laughter either. Sex seemed a determined and serious business in this place. I kept on whistling.

Returning to my cubicle, I reached into my duffel bag on the floor beside the bed and got out one of the apples I'd brought with me and lounged back and munched at it, the crisp taste freshening my mouth, cleansing the palate, so to speak.

As I was biting away at the apple, a stocky man of medium height, either sporting an early tan or naturally darkfleshed in the uncertain light, had walked up and now stood silently regarding me in the doorway. His head was clean-shaven, not a bristle on it, the top of his skull glimmering like porcelain in the vague light from the ceiling high above.

He surveyed me for several long moments. Self-conscious, I let the hand holding the apple drop to my side. With the light off in my cubicle his face was in shadow, but I could see he had a powerful build, thick-shouldered, bulging well-developed arms, his thighs showing like heavy plates of muscle just beneath the edge of his towel, the physique of a weight lifter.

I lifted my arm and, extending it, offered him a bite of my apple.

I wasn't sure, but I could sense him smiling. Then he said, all in a rush, "It would be unpropitious and intestinally disquieting to masticate even the minutest scintilla of your proffered *pomme d'amour*, which is really no tomato, I observe, but, in your hand, a love apple all the more, and the more appropriate in this instance."

Staring at him bug-eyed, I waited to make sure he was done, then said, "That's sure a mouthful for just asking you if you wanted a plain old bite of my apple."

It wasn't that funny but it tickled him because he laughed uproariously, dark shoulders shaking, laughter that sounded as if it could splinter all the flimsy partitions in the immediate vicinity.

"You look like some apples yourself. I'd rather take an enormous bite out of you," and saying this, he strode into the room and plonked himself down beside me on the bed, the girth of him making the platform bed creak like the squealing timbers of an old sailing ship in a high gale.

He tousled my hair in a rough, affectionate way, dropped his voice to a confidential whisper and breathed close to my ear, "I'm gloriously, magnificently, irrevocably and blissfully—*stoned*!"

He began stroking my arm like we'd been pals for years.

I lay back on the pillow and took another chomp out of the apple. Peculiar as he was, I was beginning to like him. My other arm reached around and rested on his shoulder. His skin felt coated with a layer of some kind of oil or grease. It felt cold and resistant, made stroking and caressing him unpleasant. I wanted to ask him what it was he had smeared on himself but thought it better not to ask. What if it was his natural skin condition? I didn't want to hurt his feelings, especially if he turned out to be a maniac. Mainly, I was afraid to sound unsophisticated—dumb, to be more plain. Probably he had anointed himself with one of those commercial products chemically designed to give off a strong musky "male" odor, like the ones that permeated the baths from top to bottom. It actually gave off the odor of dank lush growth in a swamp at low tide. Within minutes the cubicle reeked of it.

When I touched between his legs, my fingers hit the same greasy substance, slithering down to the base of his penis where I felt, in surprise, and in contrast to the rest of his cold, oleaginous skin, a tight-fitting cock ring, the hard metal of it warmed by the heat of his crotch.

When I went to reach beneath it, he seized my hand and said, like a DO NOT DISTURB sign hanging on a doorknob, "Not to denigrate the asshole, which is not only a most useful orifice, but an extraordinarily pleasurable one as well—Many's the grand barging I've had up the old canal—but, for the nonce, I'm giving my brown eye a little shut-eye. Did you know 'eros' spelled backwards is 'sore'? And that's just what I am right now from an abundance of backdoor pleasure—But is there ever such a thing as 'an abundance of pleasure'?"

Abruptly, he hoisted himself around on the bed, kicked the door shut with one foot and, snatching me by the ankles, lifted my legs as if they were pipe cleaners. He shoved his enormous back against the wall so that it shuddered under the impact, then lowered my legs and laid them across those substantial thighs of his that he'd managed to get somehow, all in the same swift action, into a surprisingly agile lotus position.

It all happened so fast I didn't have a chance to protest, or get too scared. By now I'd decided to go with the notion the bigger the he-man, the bigger the baby, and that softened some of my fears.

Right away he started to run his fingers like milers around and around my thighs, big blunt square hands they were, but the touch of them was as light as the brushings of butterfly wings. I began to relax.

"You're a nice long skinny drink of water," he said, racing his eyes up and down the full distance of me.

Despite the threat of his overpowering bulk, I said, brazen, "Take as long a drink as you want."

He looked me square in the eye, grinning. "I'm warning you, I got a powerful thirst. I'm as horny as a desert lizard."

"Drink up," I said, still cheeky. "Skinny waters run deep. Give your dowsing rod a try."

It was corny but fun, bantering this way. If he was high, it didn't seem out of control. He seemed a decent sort.

I was amazed to feel a deft magic in those thick heavy fingers that the surface nerves of the skin of my thighs instantly responded to: they leapt to life like dust-parched frogs in a flash flood.

I eased myself down onto the mattress, settling my frame into it as deep as I could, my apprehension over his strangeness, and his being so quickly intimate and proprietary, disappearing under the spell of his exact and able caresses. I gave myself over to him, trusting those strong hands with their delicate touch. It was something to see him gaze down on my body with an almost mystical concentration of regard and absorption, as though my bony physique was something marvelous he'd never seen before, even though I knew that couldn't be so.

Let me try to tell you what it was like:

His fingers continued to play over my thighs, playing like feathers around them. Then he fluttered them over my groin, like wings, fluttering them up and down. I watched my cock, as if it was a creature separate from myself, gradually awaken. The head of it appeared to move and follow, like a charmed snake, the rapid beatings of his fingers in the air above it, the sweep of them now descending close, now lifting higher, then circling around in low swoops above it, all but brushing the tip of it but never once touching. My cockhead swayed with the twitterings of his coaxing fingers like a flower swung in the currents of a breeze.

The musiclike rhythm the blunt tips of his hands strummed so precisely on my flesh made every single hair a finely tuned string under his playful and masterful fingerings; each cell a microscopic drum resounding with tiny beats of pleasure to the light tattoo of his fingers on them.

His hands moved up to my belly and he began to knead it in a particular way, with the expertise of someone who knows just where to press and how to massage it, that made me keenly aware for the first time what an area of extended erotic sensation the stomach can be.

He had such an intuitive sense of where and when and how to touch, I asked if he was a masseur, or a chiropractor. He only smiled and for an answer cupped my left hip in his huge hand and, turning it toward him, searched over it with his thumb, pressing flat against the hipbone in slow, revolving motions. Closing his eyes, he found the spot he wanted and, applying gentle pressure, screwed the flat of his thumb firmly against the skin.

I wriggled up and down on the mattress, trying to force myself out from under the strength of that single thumb boring into my hip socket, pinning me to the mattress like an object in a vise. Never before had I felt such an unbearable tickling sensation.

"Quit it!" I squealed and, the excruciating sensation of it soon bordering on pain, wrenched my hip loose from his steel-like grip.

"Sciatic nerve," he said, grinning down at me calmly, a teasing glint in his eye. Some nerve, I wanted to say, but kept quiet, knowing he was only kidding and wanting to show I was able to take a joke.

He began massaging my stomach again and that helped pacify me.

The pleasure of his sure hands there, in that way you knead dough, was reassuring, became a fanlike extension of gratification, a quiet rush of warm and sentient blood swarming up from the roots of my groin where the snake of me now raised itself to its full height and circumference, subtly tingling and pulsing with a life I had rarely felt before, even as a randy adolescent.

His finger-touchings released me into a childlike place of first-time awareness: My voice whispering, the sound of my breath in my ears, I heard as the voice and breath of a woman, quiet and assured and deep-centered, sounding more and more the whispers of a darkened stranger arising in me unbidden, growing familiar, welcome; a special tone of voice, a voluptuous grace, the woman speaking in a man's throat, the man speaking in a woman's, synchronous, neither opposing. The ears prick up to listen; my own listen. Such voices enter the mind and heart like caressings of pleasurable seduction, no less substantial or meaningful, the welcome invaders of our hearts and thoughts. Sharp, resistant angles rounding; like sometimes in strong women I see the remnants of what women used to be, before they lost their power; what they will be, awakening, again. An image of strong bare-breasted women in great rough bark canoes paddling to defend life against blind male strangulation, flashed in my mind and faded.

"There is no opposite sex."

The gestures and gyrations of my body became different, like those of another, became more spontaneously rhythmical. Totally relaxed and slowed down, yet also heightened, tensed, I discovered myself laughing from some profound part of myself I didn't know was there, had forgotten. My tongue, my throat, became dark honey, like black voices and laughter that send a thrilling ripple down the spine in their deep, throaty richness, in a wondrous and sensuous courtesy of dark blood.

He placed his mouth over my cock, his lips succulent petals folding in and out of sunlight, stalk-squeezing in fast cloud-cover, his tongue hips that swiveled up and down the stem, enlivening every straining fiber, setting every single nerve of pleasure dancing.

Pulling more and more of me deep into his throat, I felt loosened from gravity, my hips lifting weightless from his thighs, my entire body wanting to go into him, into the very heart of the hot and generous cave, contracting and expanding, that was his darkness, the circling of my being around it, blood-rooted, integral.

Without pausing, he inserted a finger in me, wriggling it sinuously upward till it touched the prostate, minnowing it in tiny curlings of massage. The stretch of my body arching over his thighs became a twisting, pulsating serpent engorged with blood.

An inward irradiation of sunshine flooded me, and on the surface of my skin, like freshening fields, a surge of renewed aliveness I hadn't known since childhood. I came as I'd never cum before, in showers. The house of my skin is a place of pleasure.

I was surprised to find I was still clutching my half-eaten apple in my hand. I held it up to show him and he laughed, another of those wall-shaking laughs. Putting his huge arms around me, he embraced my chest so tight I began to feel smothered and punched at his shoulders to let go.

The fleshy part of the fruit was turning brown, giving off an apple-scent of autumn in the close room. I again, half-serious, offered him a bite of it.

He smiled, tight-lipped, and shook his head, then gathered me in his arms and, for the first time, kissed me on the mouth.

"You know," I said, bold, "You're a terrific

cocksucker."

"I take that as a compliment!" he roared, and grabbing me in another one of his bear hugs, planted a loud wet smack on my kisser.

He tapped my chin with his forefinger and said, "I'll see you at the next Gay Pride March."

I stared at him, unbelieving. "How you going to find me, let alone remember who I am, in that big crowd?"

"If you hear somebody holler out, '*Hey, Johnny Apple-seed!*'"—his voice thundered in the tiny cubicle, giving me a start—"You'll know it's me."

"If you shout that way I can't help but hear it."

He laid a hand on my cheek, then pulled himself up off the bed, adjusting his towel around him. At the door he snapped on the light and turned around to look at me, studying my face for a few moments.

"I just wanted to be sure I'll recognize you, at the march," he said. Then, "Shall I close the door?"

I nodded.

He lifted his hand in a wave of goodbye, turned out the light and, shutting the door behind him, was gone.

I plumped up the pillow under my head, stretched out my legs and folding my hands over my chest, closed my eyes. I felt all squirrely grins inside.

With so much marijuana smoke in the air, hanging like a constant unmoving cloud in the dead-space between the actual ceiling and the partition-tops of the cubicles, I was beginning to feel a slight woozy buzz, just by simply breathing. Drifting off into sleep, some noise outside would pull me back, but then I would drift loose again, vivid, brightly colored images swimming in, sharply focused behind my closed lids.

Drowsing, I visualized affection in the air like gusty kisses, all the kisses that had ever been given here, in the air like scarlet-winged moths still beating about all the naked light bulbs in all the shabby rooms throughout the baths. They were still fluttering through the maze of halls—I could hear them sporting friskily in the black air above my cubicle.

All the hearty sighs of satisfaction, too, all the mouth smacks of unbearable pleasure, the intimate rough hand-slaps awakening flesh, and nose-nuzzlings, arousing. All the jinglings of locker and cubicle keys dangling on wrists and ankles still resounding through the labyrinth of corridors like love-bracelets and love-anklets in a music of yearning and desire, ringing, in glad surrender, the exuberant obedience we all come to. All the purposive and insistent soft padding of feet and tinkling keys, the falling whispers and rising groans from all the years up to this very afternoon and hour, flying up through the roof of the baths, swirling up and down West 28th Street, perking up the heads of the blossoms in the flower shops, circling the Empire State Building north, and soaring in a widening circle of cacophonous and sensuous rhythm and breath over all Manhattan.

Out of the roof of this neglected eros-temple of grime and sweat and steam and chlorine and antiseptic and root-sap. forced out of sunshine, out of moonshine, out of sight and hearing, pound inaudible drums and tambourines, streams of Eleusinian flowers more numerous and varied than all the cut blossoms in the wholesale floral shops; scattering playful and abandoned over the skyscrapers and steel-girded struts of bridges, high above the subway scream—blood-red flowers of affectionate delight visible only to children, and fools, and innocents, all untamed things, and the "lowliest" peoples, the simple hearts, pushed down and down, who know and never lose this fierce and savage secret, this unspeakable kindness.

And the unspeakable kindness of all those who have purified and prettied the dirt and ugliness and sneaking fear of these baths in the cleansing fertility and generosity of their erotic imaginations and desire; who, in a million small kindnesses and affectionate courtesies, have made it beautiful in spite of imposed darkness and neglect, in spite of shame and scorn and indifference and violence that makes so many of us non-things; who strive in their presence to make more lovely, against all hostile odds, these baths, this gay phoenix rising out of a nest of sweaty, fear-drenched ashes and secret, burning pain in hiding. Its rainbow speckled wings seemed to enfold the place and stretch out over the roofs of the entire block, preparing for flight, to spread the restless and generous beauty of itself far beyond the fixed skyscrapers and limits of the city.

The hate-stunted offspring of this fabulous phoenix still flitted in blind trapped flight through the maze of corridors here, flitted outside my door, wingtips batting against the confining partitions; creatures of non-opposing sex, cruisers of amorous air, messenger birds from paradise, night-flyers called "birds-of-prey" by deathpack hunters who rip their gorgeous feathers out by the roots to adorn, bloody and spine-broken, as trophies of defeat, the heads of the rippers and tramplers, sex-frightened.

I plunged into a deeper sleep and dreamed brilliantly colored geometric visions of gardens, mosaic designs of perfect and harmonious symmetry in shapes of intricate mandalas that were circles within squares, squares within circles—Gardens in multiple shades of greens and browns and yellows and whites—And grass, like grass made by artisans, richer and shinier than any I had ever seen—Precise gardens like some past secret of order and serenity.

The gardens vanished and a brilliant orange tiger, glistening black stripes rippling on the sinuous muscles of its hide, stalked down a slope in a jungle—Thousands of bright leaves hung down from the air—There was no sky, only the vivid green, almost transparent, of long hanging jungle vines and high trees in a rain-forest, giving off a luminous underwater light, each leaf separate and distinct, like seeing the first green leaves of the world. And the tiger prowling silently through it.

I felt something prodding at my cheek and awakened to discover a man standing at the side of my bed, holding the front flap of his towel aside, his erect penis staring me in the eye. He was pushing his hips impetuously at my face.

Half drowsy from sleep, cannabis hazy, and feeling amenable from my last encounter, I put it to my mouth, sliding back the skin of its sheath with a careful nudging of my front teeth. Clammy it felt, and chill, with the cold you sometimes taste, and smell, a certain sharp acidity, in fear.

He began to stab at me harder, demanding, then reached over behind me with a grim, determined look and roughly jammed a finger between my buttocks. I felt a sharp pain flare up my spine from the force and suddenness of it. Instantly he withdrew his hand, as if he had received an electric shock, and snatching me by the hair, forced my head back, releasing himself from my mouth—for which, though puzzled, I was relieved. With an expression of disgust creasing his face, he snapped his towel across his groin and stomped angrily out of the room.

Baffled, the roots of my hair still tingling from his hard yanking, I stared for a long moment out the empty doorway. A shiver passed through me, in a delayed reaction of fear.

"You blood-sucking crab," I cursed silently after him. "May you be reborn an ingrown hair sprouting around the impacted asshole of an uptight homophobe!" and immediately took it back, not wishing that on anyone, the first part anyhow.

He reminded me of many sexually brutal men I'd encountered in the past, men I searched out in dangerous places, unconsciously seeking my own internalized need for punishment and death, taught to hate myself, hating my own people, the cancerous eruption of that spreading to many. (Let this be, in small part, amends, to myself, and them, for that betrayal.)

Curious as to why he should have snatched his hand away as if he'd touched a wet wall socket, I reached down and felt myself there. It was slippery with a thick gob of lubricant. I was bewildered, not having used any so far while at the baths. It could only, of course, have been the doing of the man with the shaven head. Where he could have concealed lubricant on his body, or even under his towel without my knowing it, was a mystery to me. But he, being in my mind, a magic sensualist, was capable of anything, even, at the proper moment and without my seeing it, of magically conjuring a tube of KY out of thin air.

I expect the stranger who'd just stormed out highly insulted perhaps considered me "used" and therefore "unclean"—or, more likely, inconsiderate and unhygienic not to shower after my last enjoyment, something I'd planned to do immediately after I'd rested a bit. Some men don't mind that—it turns them on in fact—but others are more fastidious, and rightly so, without being fanatic about it.

Of course, he may have been just another testosterone-crazed male who thinks that everything comes out of the end of a penis, or the barrel of a gun, including the world.

Still, I couldn't help wondering what the fear was that gave him such a smell of fright. That negative energy also electrified the air of the baths, I could smell it now as I walked through the halls to the stairway leading down to the basement, as keen in the nostrils as the burning odor of electricity from the third rail in the subway.

I hit the showers again, taking extra time and care in cleansing myself. Then I climbed back up to the second floor, determined this time to enter the dormitory there, nicknamed the "orgy room" by the habitués of the baths.

I paused uncertain, one foot inside and one foot outside the entrance. The light in the corridor wasn't exactly bright, but the bluish light within the dormitory was practically nonexistent. There again were the row on row of beds with their pallid sheets and the barely visible figures like sprawled or sleep-stiffened corpses lying on the narrow mattresses. I hung back for a few moments, feeling safety in the meager light of the corridor. Men pushed by me, their bare arms brushing mine, as they moved in a rapid traffic in and out of the room.

Why not go in, I thought, risk it. Why spend all this time here only to leave, not knowing what it's like?

My breath quick, my heart skittering erratically like a trapped wild thing, I edged into the darkness, proceeding cautiously, threading my way along the aisle between the first row of beds, careful of my steps. As I inched along I felt something wet and slimy stick to the sole of my foot. Reaching down, curiosity overcoming repulsion, I stripped the thing off and, holding it up against the bleak light framed in the doorway from the hall, saw it was a freshly wet and wrinkled condom. I dropped it carefully out of the way at the base of one of the platform beds and continued on.

At the end of the aisle a youngish-looking man lay curled like an embryo on his side in a drugged sleep so heavy he didn't make the slightest stir or sound when others stopped at his bedside, their hands slithering like mice along his arched hip and the sleek, fully exposed curves of his buttocks. He looked himself, in his nakedness, so exposed, so vulnerable. As I approached I could smell the tart sour-mash reek of whiskey around the bed. Some men bent low over the sleeping figure, spoke close in his ear, but got no response, only his long, deep, measured breathing, mucous rasping in his throat.

I wondered if men died here, unknown and

unattended, in overdoses or convulsions, only the smell of their decomposing bodies drawing attention finally, or the fact that their twelve hours were up. How many murdered behind the locked doors of cubicles by those suffering the terminal derangement of homophobia, the commotion of the cries and struggles of the victims taken as no more than further sounds and grapplings of painful and strenuous sexual activity?

As I passed by the bed one man was forcing his face between the sleeping youth's thighs, his nose rooting, his hands trying to pry the legs apart, but the youth, so locked in paralytic sleep, kept them tightly closed, unyielding, and the man soon gave up and moved on.

At the crook in the "L"-shaped part of the room I glimpsed the same flitting figures, smudges of vapor wavering in the dense black air around several of the beds, like catafalques, in the bend of the dorm. On one, white knees were abruptly lifted high up, white thighs strained apart on the sheets, a flurry of towels beating around the bed, smoky heads darting up and down in silhouette against the chalky flesh of the elevated legs.

Not ready for it yet, I thought, and steered myself in the opposite direction, to the left, away from the orgiastic activity, to the darkest area of the dormitory.

The barely luminous flesh of a figure lying on a bed in the farthest corner where the air was blackest, was reaching its arms out to me. I moved toward it, my hands like feelers out before me, the heavy air palpable. Widening my eyes to see, to make out what the figure looked like, I stumbled against the edge of the platform bed on which it lay. Righting myself and drawing near, I was able to perceive now that the specterlike figure was a very old man, his meager white arms still stretched toward me. I took his hands, warm and dry, and clasped them in my own. He held them in a firm, passionate grip, and I thought of my own father, dead now these past three years, and how, near the end, he had held my hands in just this way.

I bent over and kissed his gummy mouth. His lips, flaccid, suctioned on mine in a surprising hold, the same firm insistence and suckling noise of a baby at a breast. One of his hands groped for mine again, the fingers, like bone, sliding into mine, and once more I felt the grasp of it as tenacious and tight as the always amazing grip and determination in a baby's fingers, holding on.

I pulled my mouth away, finally, to breathe.

Stroking the wrinkled flesh of his chest, I cupped his flabby nipples in the points of my fingers. His thin papery skin had a smell of the gradually decaying cells of the old, ripe and moldering, the fresh cells slower now to replace them.

I knelt at the side of the bed and pressed my lips to his groin, wiry dry hair, took the softness of him into my mouth. His bone-sharp hips lifted a little from the mattress, then fell back quickly from the effort. A low whistling breath escaped from his lungs.

He began to make quick motions with his arms, upward jerky thrusts. I looked at him, not understanding at first what he wanted, unable to read his face, all sunken shadows. He crooked his finger for me to stand close.

The loud snuffling of the old man as he leaned out sideways from the pillow, his face flat against me, were sounds like the slaking of a thirst, an appeasing of hunger, in the way some very old people eat with a noisy slurping, in a hearty vigor resistant to diminishing life. The strength of his appetite amazed, and assured, me.

It was in a communion of flesh we seemed to feed each other, were nourished, recharging mutual energies, stalled starveling estrangement, held death from exclusion off for one more day. Raising the blood for each other, venerable father, I thought, old nourisher, nourishing the son, the old man I would become, was the Host our bodies came feasting in momentary affection, ourselves welcoming and celebrating hosts in the house of our skin, in the meaning of Christ, mistaken and misunderstood 2,000 years.

He kissed my stomach and placed his arms around my middle. I could feel the long bones of his arms through their skin pressing my spine. I stood still and let him hold me.

There is only desire, after all; there is only, and always, need, and what we do for each other. And the rest is fear of variousness of the ways that take us, centripetal, deep and dark-rooted, in ceremonies of becoming, down to the place we all walk with common measure, on common ground, in the center, which is uncommon happiness and strength.

I bent down and kissed him on the side of the face. "Gay father," I whispered, "Thank you." He was nodding his head and I squeezed his hands, he seizing mine more tightly in return, then he let them go. I walked off down the black aisle between the row of wooden beds.

Still in that part of the dormitory where the shadows were deepest, I sat on the edge of a vacant bed, looking around, getting my bearings. A strapping baldheaded man, the large hulk of his body gleaming phosphorescent above the supine body of a big black man, a barely visible anthracite mound, coupling on a bed nearby. Both 69ing in a frontal head-to-feet reversal, the black man lying on his back, the white crouched over him, pumping into his mouth, his own face buried deep, palpitant, in the black man's groin.

Others slipping by along the aisle approached me, hands reaching out of the darkness to touch my face, my shoulders, pale hands sliding between my legs, up under my towel, a profusion of hands reaching; and half-seen faces bending close to mine, withdrawing, disappearing into the dense shady light.

Somewhere, hard to locate just where it was coming

from, the sound of splashing liquid, water sports, as they're called. Faint traces of urine and feces smell in the stale air.

A man with the sturdy squat build of a laborer, black wavy hair and, from what I could make out, a rough-featured handsomeness, thrust his bulging towel close to my face, a lump straining out from the terrycloth big enough to bust the knot. When I went to touch the cloth with my lips, he snatched the flap to one side. Still sitting on the bed, I leaned forward and, he being uncut, skinned it back for him. "She's gettin' hot," he muttered, his voice tight through clenched teeth. After a few strokes, he yanked himself away, and with a popping gesture of his thumb and finger, snapped the foreskin over it again. Flicking his towel into place, he moved off with a quick, eager gait. Several beds away he stopped at one where another man was sitting and repeated the brief ritual all over again, then departed into the shadows and I could no longer follow him.

Up near the ceiling, against a far wall, I spied the outline of a large square box, its orange eye winking feebly. Immediately "paranoid," the actuality of oppressive experience having become habitual, I wondered if it was a concealed movie or video camera, its unseen eye endlessly scanning the length and breadth of the orgy room in wide, unflinching arcs, all-seeing, indiscriminate, automatically capturing on infrared film all that went on here, twenty-four hours a day. Perhaps the owners of the baths were even profiting, pornographically, on the unsolicited and involuntary performances of all those drawn to this magnetic darkness. The possibilities for extortion, as an additional money-making sideline, given a clientele drawn from every segment of society, were unlimited.

I thought of my own eye, a free-booting spy, traveling light, in unconscious habit, as now, dispassionately imprinting for memory storage, for future imaginative use and shaping, consciously and, if lucky, with passion and accuracy, all that went on around it. But not in a deadening mechanical way, not mindlessly taping, nor, I hope, up for sale to titillate the sensationist curiosity of the have-nevers—For what then?

I also felt easier realizing, as I'd seen in other public places, that the mysterious apparatus up on the wall must be an auxiliary lighting mechanism in case the regular lights, such as they were, failed, if the juice went off unexpectedly, or if there was a fire.

Rightly or wrongly, I also felt easier in my conscience regarding my own intents, writing all this down. Sometimes I think I do this for the time when all the juice goes off.

In the bed directly across from where I sat lay what looked to be a young man, his hands folded tightly across his stomach, his long legs emphatically close together. I could just perceive the outline of his eyeglasses and the smear of a mustache. He appeared to be asleep and yet, like the youth I'd seen earlier lying in a cubicle on the third floor, he was holding himself in a catatonic rigidity and, cold in his nakedness, with only his scant towel covering him, was doing his best to keep warm.

I got up and went over and sat myself down carefully beside him, in case he really was asleep. I touched his arm and could feel the lean hardness of his biceps, stiff and unresponsive. He made no move at all and I was about to get up, not wanting to disturb him further, when, seated close to him now and able to make out his face more clearly, I could see he was quite handsome, very young, with the look of a student.

Perhaps it was because of the nebulous light, but his face and his body, which was a well-proportioned athletic physique, reminded me of someone I knew in the past, someone I couldn't pinpoint at that moment—some dream-creature perhaps. A part of my past self certainly, at least in the tightly furled rigidity in which he held himself which also gave a sense of patient waiting poised in inanimate suspension.

I touched his hands, a test to spark some awareness, even a slight signal that would tell whether he wanted me to go or stay, but his entwined fingers remained firmly locked across his belly. There was no sign that he acknowledged my presence or that I'd touched him, except that as my hand brushed down along the hair of his thighs, the stubble of it surprisingly silky—in the darkness it appeared to cover his thighs like cowboy chaps—my palm glanced off the tip of his glans, and I could feel it swelling against my skin. Glancing down, I saw the curvature of his penis draped across his thigh like a sideways banana.

I took it in my hand, making a loose fist, and began to massage it gently. I looked back at his face to see what response this had on him, but his eyes remained shut tight behind his glasses, his body held in the same position of expectant rigidity, his penis, enlarging between my fingers, the only muscle showing life.

A long scrawny arm with clawlike fingers reached across my shoulder and looking up, startled, I made out a tall figure hovering over me. The fingers of the hand coiled themselves on the youth's shoulder like an enormous spider, the lean figure stooping close, bending its head down on the pillow next to the young man's cheek.

After a few moments I realized it was the skeletal elderly man with the face of a boy I'd seen previously in the sauna. He evidently didn't recognize me in the dark, or if he did, made no sign of it, his attention focused fully on the youth.

He flung his robe open and began masturbating himself while with his other hand he started to caress the youth's hair. Stooping closer, his lips slid up and down the side of the youth's face. "You're so lovely, lovely," he was whispering in his ear, "Beautiful lovely."

As with my own nearness and touching, the young man made no move to either dissuade or encourage the older man, didn't give the slightest twitch of a muscle or flicker of an eyelid to signal any response or awareness of the other's hands and mouth upon him. I hoped the youth wouldn't rouse himself suddenly and unexpectedly in his rigor mortis and push the man away; or worse, recalling his words in the sauna, strike out at him in an abrupt fury of annoyance. But the youth did neither, lying as deathlike as before, except his penis tipped up now just above the navel.

I started to edge off the mattress, ducking my head beneath the stooping frame of the older man, relinquishing my place to him. Possessed by his terrific need, perhaps he could make better use of it, I thought. Oblivious of the unresponsiveness of the youth, his fist still worked energetically between the flaps of his gown. Whispering his string of endearments, his free hand continued to stroke the face and shoulders of the youth who, as I stood up and took one last look at him, had finally made a move: His eyes still clamped shut, he turned his face stiffly to the wall in frozen aversion.

I walked off toward the L-shaped section of the room.

At the bend in the dorm a sudden fusion of pallid bodies, arms sliding down the slopes of shoulders, curling around waists, hands clasping buttocks, pinching for ripeness, slow willowy bodies bending amid the strut and crouch of thick shoulders, the glide of the movements of dancers among the clutch and grapplings of wrestlers. Stark whiteness of towels parting, dark heads rising and falling, whiteness of towels closing like clouds over black moons of bobbing heads, opening again as if breeze-parted; towels floating on the air, floating swirling to the floor, lifted by unseen hands, knotted by invisible fingers; towels drifting off, returning, clouds of them rising and dropping light as scarves in the dark air. Whisper of bare feet on the linoleum floor. Blue robes circling at the out-skirts where I stand, glimpses of pale heavy breasts where the robes fall open at the chest. Bald heads gleaming dully. The brief glint of eyeglasses. One man lifted to a bed, his head laid back on the pillow, his writhing legs parted by a hasty grappling of hands, hands threading up and down his twisting body, heads bent to it, lips fastening over the surface of it. Two men get up on the bed, crouch between the parted thighs, one sinks to the groin, the other ducking his face further under, like someone thirsty drinking at a stream. Still on his back, his thighs now pressed flat against his chest, clutching the heels of his feet on either side of his face, he is all of an opening—one of the men moving at his nether-parts positions himself and enters. "Heaven! Heaven! Heaven!" Cries from his throat in a hoarse whisper as the cock pushes in. My eyes retreat, become plate-glass windows in the dark; my eyes reflections from the black side of the mirror.

Furry shapes approach each other in a quickening rhythm around and around the bed and in among the dark circling bodies, legs bending, extended wide, hunkering down in squats and flexings, sniffs at haunches, prance around each other, sizing each other up, heads cocked in alert; low growlings of anger, a hand slaps out at a groping figure which slinks off to the fringes of the circle.

Several heavyset men, flesh jiggling under their short blue robes, the ends of the robes flapping as they bustle through the dorm, bent intently on some unknown and mysterious but apparently important errand, hurrying in and out with surprising momentum and a composed air of urgency.

Half-moons of buttocks dimpling, spread over the low wooden wall dividing the crook in the dorm. A head swoops down out of the shadowy air, buries itself between the bearded crevice. Elbows resting on the ledge of the divider lift and drop like excited wings.

A youth stands spread-legged at the side of a bed, bucking his hips into the face of another sitting on the mattress. The one thrusting clenching fistfuls of hair, straining the throat of the other back, the seated youth gripping the thruster's thighs, his head rocking.

A tight ring of men forms around the bed to which the man has been hauled. As they watch, slow and languorous intertwining of arms and legs among them. The movement quickens, a hurrying, urgent tempo. Bodies like pale blades of petals in a sudden wind slice away from the central mass of flesh, coupling, or joining in threes and fours, drifting and sinking onto adjoining beds in an entanglement of limbs. Hands searching in blind light, grasping; pelvises rearing, sharp cries, like neighs, gasps of pleasure indistinguishable from pain.

A trickly noise of urine splashing on flesh. The abrupt rank odor of human waste.

At the peripheries, the silent watchers, stone-faced, immobile in hypnotic absorption, myself another shadow among them at the outermost boundary of the circle, my breath coming quick and dry, my heart beating like a frantic bird in my ribcage.

A black youth slipped out of the shadows and without looking at me lifted the hem of my towel and, in a sideways shifting of his head and shoulders, like a Balinese dancer, began to weave and undulate around me, turning my body with him as he turned, with gentle pullings at my towel. I had only a moment to recognize him as the youth by the swimming pool who had shown me how to adjust my keys to silence their jangling, because he then took the edge of my towel in both hands and, moving backward among the silent onlookers, tugged me, in a slow, coaxing manner, into the innermost circle of activity.

I felt the wings of the bird of my heart lift into my

arms like pinions as I placed my hands on his shoulders and followed, the youth holding the hem of my towel outstretched in his hands like a reversed train.

He led me to a bed and turning me by the shoulders, gestured that I should lie down. I placed myself on the bed, the smell of long-gone bodies rushing up to my nostrils as I sank into the mattress. He unknotted the towel from my waist and let the ends of it fall to either side of me on the sheet. He kissed my mouth in a brief flickering way.

I sensed his darkness, the air around us, smiling. His hands on me were like the way he might smooth himself when alone. His face moved close down my stomach, his tongue a belly dancer shimmying over it. I stroked his head between my hands, my fingers dreaming smoky velds, the sun-blackened brush of African mountains, caressing a continent between my fingers, the whorls of the shells of his ears like hills, like rivers. His mouth on me the wings of a rare and wonderful rain-forest bird, flitting gorgeously, irrigating desert stretches of me I hadn't dreamed were thirsty.

As others crowded around the bed, mute and unclear blacknesses hovering around, the darkness in the room became more than darkness as the black youth moved away, bearer of light and simple artifice, melting into the shadows, and another dark shape slid between my thighs, gliding his warm mouth evenly and caressingly up and down me. My shoulders turned on the pillow, my head turned, my mouth taking in a faceless stranger out of the dark. While another stranger fastened his lips at my groin, another reached under and began to massage me. The man at my head was all dark blood in my mouth. Fire-scattering meteor-tails shooting down my throat, spark-flowers blazing in my black entrails. He moved away and now there was a hand on my shoulder and I turned my head to the other side of the pillow and took another into my mouth, deepthroating, to go in, deeper and deeper, in thrustings probing for light. Unseen fingers still massaging me and another hand reaching past that hand and carefully squeezing, cupping and uncupping. Another dark form approached and swung my haunches around from the hands of the others, and up to him, putting his face to it, his wide flat tongue working, pulling himself up so that now we were both with our heads to the foot of the bed. He spit on his cock and with the wetness from his tongue there, slipped easily into me.

Now I am a woman, and now I am a man, there's no confusion. The false selves slide away in my nakedness. I am my naked self in double-energy and double-entity, and all who touch me are the same. I am berdache, not the slave-worker, defiled, but the one who ruts for corn, celebrated for slap-happy posteriors by all the bucks who enjoy them in the dance of the greening-time, who enjoy my tales, and jokes and songs. May they ever and always again—And the women and children, too, to make them laugh. All power to women and the woman in me.

Others now clustering around the bed, the fat ones in their short blue robes, their fingers busily dusting my shoulder blades, the bones of my hips, in deft caressing strokes, eager attendants in the merry service of eros, abetting; fussers and comfort-makers, obedient and devoted midwives to Priapus hurled in the pitch-black air, the force of it thumping into me like a drum all the way up to my heart and beating strong with it, another eruption of light among eruptions without number in the gloom of this huge cavernous space where no light shines in.

I felt possessed by the revelation of what must have been the secret delivered at the ancient mystery rites, at deepest night, beneath the earth, in cave-light, in the light of roots, where eros makes us make ourselves, makes us see in blindness, in sight and sense renewed in out-radiatings of spirit and flesh re-creation, in erotic circlings without hierarchy.

These faceless men surrounding me on the bed in the dorm, faces, bodies, anonymous, androgynous, were dexterous and insistent participants in the self completely subdued, impersonal; the will, the ego, falling away. To be subsumed in the will and drive of eros, to be taken in its hands and taken down and down into the nameless, faceless, anonymous dark of the flesh; to be taken down to the grit and speck of beginnings in sperm-fire and shimmering alluring dancing womb-egg; to be taken down to the salt-smell of sweat and blood and flesh and the cloacal fungus smell of buried earth and waste—To know it is all a beauty of beginning, of the sane and healthy lust that makes us all, in the primal amoeba of our infinitesimal microscopic stirrings.

And I was taken down, lost mind, self, lost self-will, taken down in that darkened dorm at the baths by the workers and dancers and servants of eros on the field of my bodyflesh, and that was a light and a revelation, and that will keep me sane and whole.

These are my roots, intact, my speck, and all my roots. No need for histories, no need to trace back further than this being taken down, in the prime and instantaneous vision of all our histories, into the speck of mindless and faceless flesh and spirit origins, the seed of the universe in the child-seed.

Let this be my history now to know what has always been; make it in this instant in a way that knows surer than any other.

Supported and held in the embracing arms and legs of these unknown men, in cupping hands like nests, I was swayed in the midst of a tree of flesh, my body, centered among them on the bed, the trunk of the tree. My off-shooting limbs intertwined among theirs, among their supportive bodies rocking me in branches of arms, were cradled in a mutual protection and nourishment of flesh, the whole of me grounded in the roots of steadying and protective skins of strangers who were no longer strange to me, who had become extensions of my own flesh, grounded in them, a taproot among other living taproots, direct and deep and secure.

The smear of faces about the bed showered up in my eyes and over and around me in a blurred spray of blossoms becoming apple buds, sending me dark apples of strength from the core of the hot black hearts pounding close to me, the sap of their blood buzzing in my ears, beating strong with my own. Their overarching bodies formed a sheltering canopy of leaf and branch and flower, their faces glistening dark fruit, the whole of it shooting up from the piss-wet floor, bowering over and around the space of the bed, momentarily dispelling the alienating greasy shadows pressing around us in the dorm.

Yes, we are fruits, we are all fruits, if we only knew, and have always been and will always be: luscious and emphatic fruits, love-plums and melons of rounding amour and succulent hanging fruits of the most delectable kind, tasty to the lips, sweet and tart in the mouth; valentine-fruits in the rightsideup and the upsidedown—Paradise lost of the doubleness we were, in the pinhead of being, acculturated splits from totality now, incomplete creatures longing, halved, the painful yearning for paradise refound, of sundered duality re-fused. The cosmic totem strength is in me, in all, held in the arms of each other, consoling and strengthening in singular regard and vitality. Perilous

     A DAY AND A NIGHT AT THE BATHS

that we begin to embrace, that we marry the woman in us, and the man.

Let me not be "Good"—Let me be fierce, bright and untamed, pitiless, with the open unblinking eyes of the Kwakiutl bird-head behind my falseface. Let me plunge in my oceans, plummet into my trees, tend to the wild gardens of myself, the wilderness forests and jungles where my untamed animals prowl, silent and sleek and singular, strong in beast-spirit, supple and curvaceous in the sprite of the unbent tendril and vine. And in the small plums that are nipples, and the apples of the thighs—Fruits are delicious—Thank eros, we are.

I was alone on the bed, all the dark shapes departed. For the time being, the room was quiet. A few men wandered in one wide doorway and out the other, passing quickly, with cautious, furtive movements through the dorm, looking around curiously but not lingering. Several yards off, in one of the aisles, a man stood, hands loose at his sides, silently watching me. Another, lying on his side, propped up on one elbow on a bed close by, was also eyeing me. Both starers were mute and quietly calculating witnesses whose faces I couldn't read. I felt no need to. Scattered here and there on other beds around me were hardly seen bundles of flesh, relaxing or sleeping, a few with arms flung out like the dead. There was the guttural sound of the quick catching of breath in sleep. In a far corner the rasp of loud snoring. Aside from that, an eerily quiet lull was in the room, like the cleansing stillness after a violent storm, presaging change. I closed my eyes and found, instead of fatigue, that I felt purified, exhilarated, and this despite the fact that my hands resting on my thighs could feel the skin sticky from the tongues and lips of all those anonymous mouths. The smell of their sweat, mingled with my own, was strong on my body and acridly sweet in my nostrils.

At length, rested, I pulled myself up off the mattress, the skin of my back peeling away from the sweaty adhesive sheets with a stinging sensation. I draped my towel loosely around me and headed toward the long flights of stairs leading down to the showers, dragging my steps, savoring the smell of their bodies commingled with mine, their sharp mineral taste in my throat, the saline dance of it strong in the pit of my belly and bowels.

Before descending the stairs, I stopped in the alcove next to the toilet where there was a water fountain and rinsed my mouth, the water cold and aching against my teeth, and spit out the residue in the urinal trough just inside the door.

In the shower room, I stood under the showerhead for a long time, the faucet turned on full-blast, letting first hot then cool streaming water pour down on me, this time oblivious to the bodies of the men showering around me, the torrential pressure of the water relaxing my spit-stiffened skin.

I needed some air and, after toweling off, right away climbed back up to the third floor as fast as I could. Once there, I headed directly down the long corridor to the little window set in the casement at the front of the building. Shoving the glass panel open as far as I could, I stuck my head through and leaned out.

Workers, homeward-bound, were scurrying along in the stiff wind in the street below, heading toward the BMT subway entrance on Broadway. I was disappointed not to see flowers in their hair. Twenty-eighth Street was clogged with rush hour traffic and the deafening beeping of horns. The air was beginning to darken a little, so I knew it must be near sundown, sometime after five o'clock.

I shut my eyes and breathed the congested air deep in my lungs a couple of times, its coldness reviving me. When I opened them again I saw the Empire State Building rearing its granite shaft and the tip of its metallically sculpted head to the sky, the architectural cap of it blush-pink, a long Revlon fingernail, in the rays of the sun going down over the Jersey Palisades. Long slanting bars of light streamed through the heavy clouds piled over the Hudson in one final wink of the day across the tenements and skyscrapers of the gritty, windswept city.

There was an erotic jest in that wink to match my own lively feeling: in its last blink of light the setting sun transformed the Empire State Building into a giant erection, ingot-red, that poked its head through the low, bare-bottomed clouds which were pink-flushed and cumulously voluptuous.

Suddenly I realized I was very hungry and, pulling myself in from the window, headed directly back down to my cubicle.

When I got there, I scrabbled around in my canvas bag and brought out a cellophane-wrapped packet of, appropriately enough, Venus Wheat Wafers ("All Natural Ingredients—No Preservatives") that I'd brought along with me, gobbled them all down with big swallows of coffee (no sugar) from my bike thermos, ate another apple (Delicious), then tucked myself up on the bed for a little snooze.

Snatches of surrounding voices flying in the air: "Stick it *in*, stick it *all* in, *ram* it up there." "Hurt me—hurt me more—*more*!" The crack of poppers snapped like mini-firecrackers from nearby cubicles. But the words, the sharp sounds, the animal cries and pantings, had no meaning to me; far off sounds from another distant place. I was afloat in a deep and quiet peace of intactness, like after the long raging of a high and insidious fever subsiding, the body drained of its poisons.

Over the loudspeaker at the attendant's station crackled the staticky voice of the clerk from the check-in window in the downstairs lobby, "234, his time's up," and the attendant's bark in reply, "Room 234, ri-i-i-i-ght!" A different Puerto Rican voice this time, so the other attendant must have gone off duty.

Voices, sounds faded, became more distant. I knew my own time would soon be up but first I needed to take a short nap before leaving. I dropped into a quick black sleep.

I was awakened by the sense of a presence close to my bed. My face, twisting on the pillow, brushed damp rough terrycloth. Opening my eyes, groggy, thinking myself dreaming, I saw standing in the half-light looking down at me with a calm and serious scrutiny the honey-haired youth I'd seen down in the showers several hours earlier. A rush of blood swelled my heart.

I couldn't see those eyes clearly, but the sea-green glisten of them was still sparking in my memory, sparked in the shadowy room.

I jerked myself up on my elbows, alert. How long had I slept? "You know what time it is?"

"Must be around midnight." His voice had a drowsy murmur. His hand was stroking my shoulder in a lazy, insouciant way.

I let my head fall back on the pillow and rubbed at my eyes. "I can't stay much longer. I got to get out of here pretty soon."

He didn't say anything. Instead, he slipped the knot and let his towel drop to the floor. Then he climbed up onto the bed, kneeling between my legs and, clasping a hand around the back of my neck, lifted my face to his groin.

The broad-lipped tip and muscular shaft sprang alive with a suddenness that quickly filled my mouth, the curvature of his blood-swollen glans, and the musk of it, like the velvety cap of a swelling mushroom in rain.

He pulled my shoulders up and I hitched my legs around on the mattress and tucked them under me, kneeling in front of him. We were now facing each other, on our knees, embracing. His enfolding arms slid down my sides as he crouched over in a knee-squat, his tongue flicking between my legs. I bent my head down and kissed the nape of his neck. The ringlets of dark blond hair had a smell of sweat and cigarette smoke. I rested my chin on his shoulder, watched his shoulder blades working, like scissoring knives of flesh, the muscles of his back rippling, the snaking curve of his spine. His lean hips flipped from side to side. His mouth was the nibblings of fish.

I lifted myself over him, my face moving down his back, tracing the musculature of it with the arrow-tip of my tongue. Tremors of flesh pulsated up into my mouth, tingled to the base of my throat. Blond wheat of hair at the small of his back, electric under the point of my tongue like the fur of a small wild creature. I extended my torso in a long arc over him to the base of his spine, arriving at the crevice, the spread slopes skin-tinted the flush of dawn, its anus the curled petals of a dark rose, sensitive petal-lips I kissed with my own.

And in the yoke below, hair with the roughness of bark scraping the buds of my tongue, the sapling-thick cord of the roots of him beginning to shake, supple and undulant against the whippings of my tongue, his testes ripening fruits lifting, the hem of their sack of pink skin, dimpled as rind, wrinkling scallops of flesh as they rose to bursting.

I swiveled my hips around, careful, not leaving him, and flung my face under, positioning between his thighs, the sap in my own roots starting to race, my lips shutting over him just at the exact instant, the beaks of our mouths bees in pollen-heavy blossoms.

We slipped over, turned on our sides, and lay quiet, lips still stem to stem, a slow murmur of golden motes twinkling behind my shut lids, the taste of him salt-honey in my throat. He smelled like sunlight.

We lay this way for some time, the room black, the shadow of his lap my head rested in, black; and yet I was basking in a light that seemed to stream from his flesh, like a part of the sun he had carried with him here from whatever margin of the sea he lived by, brightening the darkness of the place wherever he went. It brightened my eyes like noon.

I wanted to tell him this, but that might've spoiled it, so I kept quiet and carefully maneuvered myself around and snuggled up close to him, kissing his throat. We stayed pressed in each others arms for several moments longer. Then he said, "I'd ought to be going, too." He sighed contentedly. "It's been a long day."

"This was a nice way to end it," I said.

It hit me that it really didn't matter that I would probably never lay eyes on him again: the sea in his eyes and the salt-bite of him, the light he radiated that illuminated me in these brief moments, would stay with me, lighten me in dark days. I could hold all the unexpected visitations throughout my day here, like gifts, always, in any dark times to come.

He rolled off the bed with a yawn and a kick of his legs, picked up his towel off the floor and tied it firmly about his hips. Touching his brow with two fingers, he gave me a quick smile, and when he went out the door it was like a light turned off, the cubicle darker than it had ever been all throughout that day.

I jumped off the bed and hurried to the toilet down the hall to take a quick piss and for a fast water-gargle of the throat, then bounded two at a time down the stairs to the showers for one last fast wash, bounded back up to my cubicle again and struggled quick into my clothes, my time nearly up and it getting late, much later than I thought I would stay, and didn't want to get stuck paying for additional time since I had to watch my bucks.

I dropped my damp, and well-used, towel on the bed (as the crudely printed signs on the hall walls directed) and, beginning to sweat in my winter coat and sock hat, ran a swift hand over the rumpled sheets, giving one fast final look around to see if I'd forgotten anything. Slinging the duffel bag over my shoulder, I reached for the light switch and among the scrawls of graffiti and names and dates scratched in the paneling around it, one crudely etched phrase caught my eye: "I had a good time here." I nodded, switched off the light and, just before closing the door to lock it, blew a goodbye kiss to Room 208.

As I walked down the hall, past the men lounging against either wall with their quiet appraising glances or steady, rapacious eyes, feeling myself, clothed in my winter outfit, no longer now a part of it, I noticed that the door to the Oriental lad's cubicle was shut. Had he left? Or was he still there, on the other side of the wall, lying on his bed, naked, staring up bitterly at the smoky ceiling? More than likely another had already rented his space, just as they would rent Room 208, quite soon after I left.

If he was still there, I hoped that he wasn't alone, that he was with someone who was treating him well, that he would let whoever it was treat him with affection, with whatever it was he needed.

Despite the late hour, the lobby was bustling with activity: some newcomers were undressing in the locker room, men in towels were crisscrossing the lobby or queuing up at the two pay phones in the corner, some were swinging in and out of the half open dutch-door to the snackshop (I would stop in there next trip to see what it was like) or marching up and down the stairs leading to the pool and steam and sauna rooms.

There was a line-up of new arrivals with their overnight bags and canvas shoulder bags at the check-in window. A man with a gray meaty face, thick glasses and flat, unwashed-looking hair the color of pig iron was now on duty behind the glass. I got in line and waited my turn to hand in my keys and get back my belongings.

When I reached the window, the clerk pushed a slip of white paper at me through the slot. On it, scribbled in pencil, was: "TIP FOR RUIZ 25¢" I scratched my head, uncomprehending, but slid a quarter anyway back under the window from the change I'd kept with me in my levi pockets. Not knowing who "Ruiz" was, I imagined he was one of the attendants on the second floor, perhaps the one who came on duty later.

After I gave him the keys, the clerk slid out the narrow metal drawer with my wallet and watch in it. I strapped on the watch, checked my wallet and, hoisting the bag again, made one final dodge among the busy throng of towel-clad men, walked down the broad marble steps and pushed open the door that I'd entered so many hours before.

I was expecting it and yet I was surprised to see the night, like coming out of a long movie you went into in daylight. Because of the late hour the street was pretty quiet. There were a couple of pedestrians marching against the raw wind off toward Sixth Avenue. An occasional taxi jolted by at high speed. The weather had cleared. I breathed in the cold snappy air.

Over the tenements the Empire State Building, still floodlit each night in red, white and blue searchlights, commemorating last year's Bicentennial of the nation, gleamed like a rocket mock-up out of a technicolor movie where the colors aren't quite true, nor the set either.

Above and high beyond its garish beacon swirled stars flung open-handed like diamonds, real and hard and forever, in the midnight-blackened sky. I stood in the doorway of the baths and saluted them, then, twirling my scarf around my neck against the wind, stepped briskly down the sidewalk, heading toward Broadway and the entrance to the subway station.

Dedicated to the nine who died,
and to those injured,
and to those present,
in the fire that destroyed the Everard Baths
on West 28th Street in Manhattan on the morning
of May 25,1977.
And, out of the ashes and ruin of all despair,
and in spite of it,
to the spirit of the rainbow gay and lesbian phoenix, rising.

AFTERWORD

By the time I wrote *A Day and a Night at the Baths* in 1977, an explosion in queer visibility had been occurring in America since the Stonewall Inn rebellion of June 1969, particularly in the larger cities of New York and San Francisco and Los Angeles. Along with that explosion came, literally, a tremendous release of homoerotic energy, energy pent up for decades, centuries, really, when men-loving-men and women-loving-women had been furtive, hidden in shadows and shame. Same-sex eros may have been long exiled to the secret places at the fringes of society, but despite that—such is the power of eros—it managed not only to survive but to thrive, as Walt Whitman sang:

"In paths untrodden,
 In the growth by margins of pond-waters,
 Escaped from the life that exhibits itself...
 No longer abash'd, (for in this secluded spot I can
                respond as I would not dare elsewhere),
 Strong upon me the life that does not exhibit itself, yet
                contains all the rest,..."

Yes, eros survived and thrived not only for Whitman but for multitudes, despite those centuries of shame and fear, in spite of the spiritual and mental deformities imposed by religion, by imprisonment, by fear of execution, by psychiatry, by the suffocating closet. The queer spirit had a vital if hidden existence, surviving centuries of state and religious persecutions that sought to hobble and murder it—and that still do to this day.

But not as lethally. Not as lethally because what is brought visible into daylight, what is spoken aloud in earshot of all ("the unspoken becomes the unspeakable," said poet Adrienne Rich, and that has been the silent curse), spoken in all its ordinariness and extraordinariness, defuses the smothering power of enforced invisibility, of enforced silence. In the 1950s and particularly after 1969, many faggots and dykes all over America were no longer complicit in their own oppression, were no longer enablers of a severely enforced heterosexism ("Extreme heterosexuality is a perversion," said anthropologist Margaret Mead), were no longer internalizing centuries-old legalized Judeo-Xtian homophobia and traditional ignorance, were no longer locked in the cells of self, serving as their own judge, jury and executioner. The anti-queer, gender- and numbers-obsessed institutions of state and religion ("If God is male then male is God," said radical feminist and professor Mary Daly) no longer had to do the oppression—we did it to ourselves. This is the psychological mechanism that operates in internalized misogyny and racism, the same self-hating that keeps us fractious, factious and fighting among ourselves, exploiting and oppressing each other and, worst of all, keeping us separate from one another in a terrible and powerless isolation.

Before Stonewall, the gay bar, dangerous as it was, where police raids and arrests were common, was mainly all we had. The gay bar has a long history in the United States (even Whitman had Pfaff's underground in lower Manhattan in the 1850s: "—The vault at Pfaff's where the drinkers and laughers meet to eat and drink and carouse.../Beam up—Brighten up, bright eyes of beautiful young men!..."). For a long time it was the only public place where we could meet and mingle, be comfortable among our own kind, our kin, despite its being breeding grounds for alcoholism and other drug addictions, despite, as such bars increased in number after World War II, the police raids that could occur at any moment, raids motivated by ambitious politicians exploiting homophobia for their own political ends, by crooked cops greedy for pay-offs and able to justify their existence and show they were "on the job" by making easy arrests, while at the same time meeting their monthly arrest quotas, easier than going after real criminals, the equally shadowy underworld figures that owned the lucrative gay bars and whose bribes so many vice cops readily accepted.

When the black and latino drag queens, the leather dykes, the despised street queers, the "disreputable dregs" of the homo underworld who were persona non grata in the "respectable," uptight uptown homosexual bars, who had nothing to lose, stood up and fought back against the police raiders in the Stonewall Inn on that June evening in 1969 (it was a dyke who first stood in the doorway that night), little did any of us, in our wildest dreams, imagine that it would ignite a revolution that would rock the world.

And so it has.

After centuries of silence, not only were our tongues loosed at last to shout the love that had for so long dared not speak its name, shouted out loud in revolutionary meetings, zaps, demonstrations and celebratory pride marches, our tongues also were given ever more freedom to exercise themselves in another explosion of erotic caressings in intimate places, of erotic innovations set loose once the fetters were off.

Out in the open, we set ourselves to inventing ourselves with a vengeance, freeing ourselves of the old constricting het models—the religiously, criminally, psychiatrically and socially constructed Sodomite and Homosexual ("Homophobia," recently wrote lesbian author Sarah Schulman, "is a pathological manifestation of heterosexual culture...."), were becoming the gay male and lesbian, the faggot and dyke, the queer—epithets of terror embraced to defuse their ugliness and hatred—while rigid, death-ridden, politically exploitative gender was turned on it ear, as the cross-dresser came into her/his own, the leather man and lipstick dyke, the transsexual, even the clone— the possibilities of invention of queerself were endless, as were the ways for us to be together and be as families. For the first time in eons, we were naming ourselves, defining ourselves, and most important reinventing ourselves, becoming at last more an open people among the peoples of the world.

The revolution was not only in the open behavior but in the identity, and the insistence on it, the insistence to create ourselves, and how we would be with each other in the places we were.

And it goes on, the many in one, the endless possibilities: "the life that...contains all the rest..."

But at that time, in those heady days of first freedom (the wondrousness of being in the thick of the beginning of things!), when anything and everything seemed possible in the bars, the backrooms, and the baths, in the parks and along the piers, in the discos, there was unleashed in gay males at least (having, like most males, more latitude and money than most lesbians or other women) a sexual openness that had the excitement and fervor of the newly discovered pubescence in any adolescent boy. The theme song of the hour might very well have been: "Anything Goes." And it did, wherever a tongue, wherever a fist, a prick, could go, it went, and usually in the most inventive ways.

But while all that was going on, unbeknownst to us, as we screwed greedily, joyously with abandon in our dark backrooms and bathhouses, on our piers and in our discos, a microscopic organism had begun to invade many of us, up mainly through that exquisite slip of pleasure, slipping invisibly into our bloodstreams and slowly taking our lives away, as mercilessly as any medieval inquisitor.

My own attitude at the time, like so many lusty sex-positive gay males (our own innocence, really; how could we envision that sex-positive would become HIV-positive in so many thousands of us?), was exemplified by the surprise, and disgust, of the narrator in *A Day and a Night at the Baths* when, once he dared step into the orgy room for the first time, he says, "I felt something wet and slimy stick to the sole of my foot. Reaching down, curiosity overcoming repulsion, I stripped the thing off and, holding

     A Day and a Night at the Baths

it up against the bleak light framed in the doorway from the hall, saw it was a freshly wet and wrinkled condom. I dropped it carefully out of the way at the base of one of the platform beds and continued on...."

At that moment in the story, I, in the persona of the narrator, was actually more surprised than disgusted, thinking smugly, Whoever needs a condom here? Rubbers were for het males to prevent knocking up females, not for gay guys. I never used a condom in the baths—or in the backrooms or on the docks; not one of my sexual partners in those days ever used one. In fact, I never saw another condom in the baths in all the years after that. Like impetuous boys, ignorant of sexual hygiene as a result of being raised in a sex-negative society where it was never taught (and largely still isn't), we wanted nothing to come between us and our new-found pleasure, not even a thin sheath of latex (that was a breeder's worry); like impetuous boys, booze and drugs didn't help us to take precautions either; like impetuous boys, in our first rush of heady freedom, we thought we were immortal.

Even so, the narrator of *A Day and a Night at the Baths* expressed his concerns, if only momentarily:

"I imagined the sheets, the skimpy mattress, enseamed with lice, 'cooties d'amour,' as they are called, love bugs. The shapely posteriors parading by in the hall I imagined rampant with hepatitis, the penises that flamed with passion flaming with spirochetes as well; and scabies, and yaws, and all the other parasites carried here, along with desire, by the sailors of love from every port of the globe, the lonely and flesh-hungry from every corner of the nation and from every borough in the city; carrying here centuries-old infections of the fathers, their gay sons infected hosts, carriers in blind desire of invisible flesh-eating stowaways on bodies innocent of contaminating, and, in imperative yearning, riding out the fears of infection, driven to this contagious harbor again and again, myself among them now...."

But those ancient infections, for all their nuisance and terror, were curable and were nothing compared to the hitherto unknown and insidious invaders, for which, once named, there was and still remains no cure. Who could have envisioned these other "invisible flesh-eating stowaways [in] our bodies...."? (In the preceding passage, I could just as well have been writing about HIV infection and AIDS in 1977; unwittingly, in hindsight, I was.) Smugly, we thought all we had to worry about in those days were crabs and VD, and if those touched us, a trip to the gay health clinic or the good gay doctor would soon cure it: "...what with A-200 and other drugstore lice-killers, and the Gay Men's Health Project in Greenwich Village ('Free V.D. Examinations 691-6969)'). After the pleasures of Venus (and certainly Priapus), trust to the availability of penicillin...."

Even our medical phone numbers had a gay, insouciant

air....

As the years have passed, I can count back to a long list of the dead, all friends and acquaintances. It is an old refrain now among so many of us; it amounts almost to a grim obsession, the body count that each of us keeps numbered in our memory. For me, the first friend to die was Tom McCluskey at 35, in 1984; then, Steve. There were dozens in between, and as I write, many more are dying all over the globe and no longer mainly gay males, gender, age or sexual identity no barrier to the virus, the politicians, including religious politicos, just as they did in the bar- and baths-raiding days, just as they've done for centuries, still playing politics with our lives.

I stopped going to the baths in 1982, after the first terrifying rumors became increasingly undeniable facts, when I could no longer live with my rationalizations to continue my pleasures in those "eros-temple[s] of grime and sweat and steam and chlorine...," if I wanted to stay alive.

I remember saying to novelist and critic Richard Hall at the time, "The party's over," echoing the sentiments of a growing number of others. There were those, though, who could not leave the celebration and who stayed too long. Richard, sadly, was one of them, succumbing to AIDS in the mid-1980s.

Early on in the plague (for that is rapidly what it became), after the first horrors, the first denials, began to wear off, when the virus and means of its transmission were identified, we began, to our credit, to learn some things we'd never known before. We learned to protect ourselves. More and more of us learned to care for and to respect each other, to care for our sick and dying and to protect and support the living. In those early days, embattled from all sides and often alone with each other—except, to their credit, for those compassionate lesbians who became willing helpers—all the while, in the face of fierce and unrelenting enemies beyond the disease, we tried to hold the ground we had gained.

It is better today. We are still embattled on most fronts, but we are not so alone. We have made some allies along the way. And although no cure is in sight, there are today at least a few medications and procedures available to sometimes ease and prolong the lives of people with AIDS. We know, too, that in spite of the virus, we can still be intimate, still be loving, because we have found ways to enjoy each other's company that can still include the sexual, if we so choose—Because, again to our credit, we have not fallen into the trap of a society that uses the virus to entrench ever more deeply its long and maliciously imbecilic history of erotophobia, erotophobia that has estranged everybody from each other. More and more we have become loving and vitally connected partners in this unpredictable business of life, and continue to see eros as the blessed gift it is; to have grown up enough to realize there are no guarantees.

To our credit…It's time we took some for ourselves.

Michael Rumaker